Grace Livingston Furniss

A Box of Monkeys

And other Farce-comedies

Grace Livingston Furniss

A Box of Monkeys
And other Farce-comedies

ISBN/EAN: 9783744782807

Printed in Europe, USA, Canada, Australia, Japan

Cover: Foto ©Andreas Hilbeck / pixelio.de

More available books at **www.hansebooks.com**

A BOX OF MONKEYS

AND OTHER

Farce=Comedies

BY

GRACE LIVINGSTON FURNISS

NEW YORK

HARPER & BROTHERS, FRANKLIN SQUARE

1891

CONTENTS.

A BOX OF MONKEYS.

CHARACTERS.

EDWARD RALSTON... *A promising young American, half owner of the Sierra Gold-Mine.*

CHAUNCEY OGLETHORPE..... *His partner, second son of Lord Doncaster.*

MRS. ONDEGO-JHONES...........*An admirer of rank.*

SIERRA-BENGALINE..........*Her niece, a prairie rose.*

LADY GUINEVERE LLANDPOORE...*An English primrose, daughter of the Earl of Paynaught.*

Costumes—Modern and appropriate.

PROPERTIES.

1ST ACT.

Letter for Mrs. Ondego-Jhones. Writing materials. Chewing-gum for Sierra. Two sofa pillows. Paper of "light society talk." Bag and umbrella for Guinevere. Letter for Chauncey. Parcel for Mrs. Ondego-Jhones. Cigarettes and matches. Newspaper for Chauncey.

2D ACT.

Newspapers on table. Afghan on sofa. Pack of cards. Fan. Properties for charade. Letter for Mrs. Ondego-Jhones.

The charade may be elaborated, or given simply as written. But it should be kept within the limitations of an impromptu affair given in a private house, with properties and costumes hastily collected.

A BOX OF MONKEYS.

ACT I.

AFTERNOON.

SCENE. — *Drawing-room of* MRS. ONDEGO-JHONES'S *residence*, 900 *Fifth Avenue. Piano right. Sofa left. Table, with writing materials, right centre. Entrances—centre, right, left. Window left of centre entrance. Portières, pictures, chairs, etc., in handsome modern style.*

Curtain rises on MRS. ONDEGO-JHONES *at table, reading letter.* SIERRA *at piano, playing.*

MRS. ONDEGO-JHONES (*laying down letter*). Very gratifying! Very kind of her ladyship. Sierra! Sierra! (*Turns to* SIERRA; *gets up; shouts in her ear.*) Sierra!

Sierra (*jumping up*). Yes, aunt.   I think so too.

Mrs. O. You are strangely absorbed, miss. Pray, of what were you thinking?

Sierra (*innocently*). Ted—er—I mean—

Mrs. O. Is *Ted* a musical term?

Sierra. I said ped, aunt.   Short for pedal, you know.

Mrs. O. (*eying her severely*). You are sure?

Sierra. Quite sure.   (*Aside.*) That's four fibs since breakfast.   Oh, me!

Mrs. O. Very good.   Listen to this.   First sit down.   Never stand in that awkward style again.   When will you learn repose?   (*Sits by table.*)

Sierra. Can't say, aunt.   Drive on.   (*Sits sideways on her chair, propping her chin on her hands.*)

Mrs. O. Drive on!   But what can one expect from a girl brought up by a man on a ranch?   However, listen, Sierra.   I have here a most gratifying letter from the Countess of Paynaught.   Her ladyship accepts, in the most friendly style, my offer of hospitality, and proposes to leave her daughter, Lady Guinevere, in my care, while she continues her tour west-

ward. Ah! little did I think when I made my
offer on the steamer that her ladyship would
confide her daughter to me for the winter.
Quite an honor, isn't it, Sierra?

SIERRA. Honor! I think it's beastly cheeky!
You told me yourself that her *ladyship*
snubbed you persistently from Liverpool to
New York, and called you that Ondego-Jhones
person.

MRS. O. Her ladyship's manner on the
steamer, Sierra, was due to a contest between
a plebeian ailment and an aristocratic diges-
tive apparatus. In short, her ladyship was
sea-sick. No one dreams of making sea-sick
people accountable for anything they say.

SIERRA. I don't care! I would not have
her daughter.

MRS. O. (*absently*). How well it will sound!
Among other distinguished visitors were Mrs.
Ondego-Jhones and her guest, Lady Guinevere
Llandpoore. Delightful! I rather think that
will take down Mrs. Newcome, who is insuffer-
able on the strength of her puny little Italian
count. The idea of my entertaining members
of the English aristocracy will simply annihilate her.

(SIERRA *becomes absorbed in seeing how far she can stretch her chewing-gum.*)

MRS. O. Lady Guinevere arrives to-day ; she can assist at Sierra's début to-morrow. I will write the notices for the society notes. (*Writes.*) "Mrs. Ondego-Jhones introduced her fascinating niece, Miss Sierra Bengaline, at a *Kaffeeçlash* yesterday afternoon. This German innovation proved a pleasant relief from the monotonous 'teas' in vogue." (*Aside.*) That's a slap at Mrs. Newcome's weak tea. (*Writes.*) "Lady Guinevere Llandpoore, only daughter of the Earl of Paynaught, assisted in receiving. Miss Bengaline, who was brought up in the distant West, brings the spicy atmosphere of her native prairies with her." I put that in, Sierra, to account for any atrocious thing you may see fit to do.

SIERRA. Good idea.

MRS. O. (*writes*). "Miss Bengaline was the recipient of numerous bouquets"—(*aside*) I shall order nine this morning—"and bids fair to be the belle of the season." (*Lays down pen.*) There, that will do, when the gowns are described and the names added. Now I must fly to the intelligence-office, and secure at least three maids before lunch. Sierra, what do I see? Remove that vile stuff from your mouth, and sit up.

SIERRA. Yes, aunt. (*Sticks the wad of gum on back of chair; sits up primly.*)

MRS. O. Pay attention! The butler Mrs. Campbell recommended is to come this morning. You will have to open the door and interview him. It looks dreadfully, but can't be helped, since cook is the only servant who didn't "strike" yesterday. Well, ask this man the usual questions, and, if he is at all presentable, engage him. (*Bell rings.*) Gracious! Is it possible Lady Guinevere has arrived? Run to the window and see.

SIERRA (*runs to the window; looks out; turns to audience*). It's Ted, and aunt not gone. I'll beckon him to go. (*Waves her hands; shakes her head violently.*)

MRS. O. (*who has been collecting letters, eyeglasses, gloves, etc., turns, and sees* SIERRA *gesticulating*). What are you doing? Think of the neighbors! Who is it?

SIERRA (*hastily drawing curtains and coming down front*). It's no one, aunt.

MRS. O. (*severely*). What do you mean by making a—a semaphore of yourself for *no one?*

SIERRA. I meant no one in society, aunt. It was a—er—a kind of—er tramp, and I waved my hands to signify displeasure, and he went away.

MRS. O. I presume he thought you were a lunatic.

SIERRA. Yes, aunt. Auntie, if that English girl is coming to-day, don't you think you ought to hurry and get some servants? She won't believe your entire staff left in a fury; she'll think you never had any. The English are so supercilious, you know.

MRS. O. Yes, yes, I'm off. Don't forget about the butler, Sierra. (*Starts towards centre door; comes back.*) And, Sierra, con over that little abstract I made for you of light society talk. I don't want a tongue-tied débutante on my hands.

SIERRA. What a nuisance!

MRS. O. Nonsense! A girl has to work for popularity nowadays. Well, good-bye. (*Kisses her. Exit* c.)

SIERRA. I thought she would never go.

Now I will beckon Ted in. (*Runs to window; looks out.*) Heavens! They nearly ran into each other. It's lucky aunt don't know him by sight. She is glaring out the window as the carriage turns the corner, and he is coming up the steps. I'll let him in. Isn't he a daisy? (*Exit c.; returns with* EDWARD RALSTON *muffled in a large ulster.*)

SIERRA. Ted, how could you ring the bell when there was no red book in the window? I had to tell aunt you were a tramp.

TED (*laughing*). I quite forgot the red book. The fact is— Look at me, Sierra! (*Throws off ulster. Shows he is in evening clothes.*)

SIERRA. Evening clothes in the morning! Oh! Oh, I see! Locked out.

TED (*indignantly*). Jove! Locked out! Nothing of the sort. I got up early, rushed off to have a picture taken in this rig to please you, and you reward me by the most injurious suspicions. I was never locked out in my life.

SIERRA. Always locked in?

TED. Sierra—

SIERRA. There, there, I won't tease any more, Ted. Don't let us spend our precious time in quarrelling. Come, sit down, look pleasant and perfectly natural, and you'll see a little bird — that's me — with some news. (*They laugh; sit on sofa, left.*)

TED. Now for the news, you little witch.

SIERRA. You remember the Countess of Paynaught?

TED. No, I don't.

SIERRA. You do, Ted.

TED. I do not, Sierra.

SIERRA (*firmly*). You *do*, Ted. She's that disagreeable woman who called aunt the Ondego-Jhones person.

TED. Oh, I recollect! you told me about her. Well, what comes next?

SIERRA. Her daughter comes next. After insulting aunt for three thousand miles, her ladyship kindly invites her daughter to spend the winter with her—*the Ondego-Jhones person!*

TED. That's rather cool. I suppose your aunt regularly flattened her out — on notepaper. Declined the honor with freezing sarcasm, eh?

SIERRA. On the contrary, she is delighted, because the wretched girl has a title, and will look well in print. She will arrive to-day, and assist at my début to-morrow. Ted (*jumps up; seizes sofa pillow*), I detest society! I feel parboiled, smothered in it. And I—don't —want—to—*come*—out! (*Emphasizes each word with a thump on the sofa.*)

TED (*springing up*). Great Julius Cæsar! Sierra, I'm not society.

SIERRA (*laughs; walks to table*). You! You're only a cowboy. Papa said so. Ted, shall you ever forget that dreadful afternoon when you rode over thirty miles to tell me you loved me, and papa found us spooning in the corral, and raved around, denouncing and cutting off, etc.?

TED (*going to her*). No; and I sha'n't forget how you stood up and defied him, like a brick—er—angel.

SIERRA. *Brick* angel?

TED. No, no; angel.

SIERRA. Oh, *plain* angel!

TED. No; like a fascinating little cherub with a good firm will of its own. Jove! how your eyes flashed when you said he might send you East, but you'd never, *never* give up Ted. (*Takes her hand.*) Sierra, I often wonder why you like me.

SIERRA (*coquettishly*). Why? Let me see. Well, you're very warm-hearted.

TED (*edging nearer*). That's so.

SIERRA. And I like your taste in — er— girls, and the shape of your nose, and you named your gold-mine after me, and I'm so sorry it will not pan out. That's it. It's pity.

TED (*putting his arm around her*). Pity, Sierra?

SIERRA (*disengaging herself, runs to other side of table*). Gracious, Ted! don't put your arm around me, and say "Sierra" in that tone. It—it makes me nervous. (*Picks up papers.*)

TED (*walking up and down*). You took it coolly enough out on your father's ranch. Of course I was a fool to expect to hold you to our engagement. I'm only a poor fellow with a gold-mine which won't pan out, confound it!

SIERRA. Oh, Ted!

TED. I see it all. To-morrow your aunt presents you to society, where you may meet some really eligible fellows. I knew there was something wrong when you didn't kiss me this morning.

SIERRA. Of course I didn't.

TED. Why of course? (*Stops in front of her.*)

SIERRA (*mischievously*). I wasn't invited.

TED (*rushing to her*). I'll take that kiss with interest, now.

SIERRA (*skipping round the table*). No, no! Please, really, Ted! I'm—I'm busy. (*Dips pen in ink, holds it out theatrically.*) One step nearer, villain, and I ink your immaculate bosom. But (*shyly*) if you'll give me a little time, I'll surely pay you.

TED. Honor bright?

SIERRA. Honor bright! Now Ted, help me get up my "light society talk." You see, aunt is so afraid I shall say something original and paralyze her "set" to-morrow, that she has forbidden me to say "mustang," "ranch," or "poker," and prepared a few well-bred inanities for me to sling at the effete East.

TED. Is "sling at the effete East" one of them? (*Takes paper from* SIERRA.)

SIERRA. Oh, I'm using you as a safety-valve! Now you go out, then come in with a hee-haw languid manner, don't you know, and I'll receive you Eastern style.

TED. All right.   (*Takes out ulster, hat ;
goes out ; comes back.*)   Ready.

SIERRA. Wait till I am posed.   (*Stiffens
herself ; crosses her hands ; holds her head on
one side ; smiles.*)   Ready, Ted.

TED (*coming forward with affectation of lan-
guor, his eyes half shut*).   Aw — chawrming
day, Mrs. Ondego-Jhones.   You always have
chawrming days *on* your days.   Is that
chawrming girl your niece ?   Present me,
pray.

SIERRA. Good !   You don't look as though
you knew enough to come in out of the wet.
Ted, I'd no idea you could look so swell.

TED. There's the making of a fine idiot in
mesilf, miss.   Proceed.

SIERRA. Now I'm to look at you composedly, but not boldly, and say, archly, " May I
give you some tea, Mr. Emtehed ?"

TED (*looking at paper*).   Then we have a
little fire of epigrams about cream and sugar,
and I ask you if you care for the opera.

SIERRA (*talking very fast*).   I'm devoted to
Wagner — (*Aside.*) What a fib ! — but care
little for the Italian school.   However, everything is so new to me—Oh, Ted, let's drop it !

TED. I'm agreeable.

SIERRA. And, Ted, I'm afraid you'd better go. Aunt may return.

TED. Go! Why, I've just come. Besides, your aunt has never seen me. I only figure in her mind as an undesirable lover named Edward Ralston. Very good; if she returns, we'll brazen it out. Say I'm a long-lost cousin or a book agent.

SIERRA. You'll have to do the fibbing, Ted. I've told five fibs since breakfast, and my conscience aches.

TED. I'll attend to it. And now I'll settle up our account: fifteen minutes' interest on one kiss makes—

SIERRA. You can't collect it.

TED. Oh! can't I?

SIERRA. First catch your hare.

(*They dodge about stage.* SIERRA *snatches up sofa pillow; runs out, followed by* TED, *They run in* R., *out* L., *in* C., *out* R.)

SIERRA (*coming in cautiously*, R.). He missed me up-stairs. I'm going to hide in the back hall, and when he comes I'll let this fly. (*Tiptoes off*, C.)

TED (*stealing in*, L.) Not here! (*Takes slumber-pillows off of chair.*) Now, then, look out, Sierra. (*Tiptoes off*, L.)

(*Bell rings violently three times. Enter* LADY GUINEVERE LLANDPOORE *in travelling gown. She carries dressing-case, umbrella, and mackintosh. Speaks in timid, hesitating style.*)

LADY G. Ahem! Is anybody home? (*Comes forward; looks all about.*) No one here. What a funny house! I rang, and rang, and *rang*. No one came. The cabby —I mean *cabman*—wouldn't wait. I couldn't sit on the steps like a beggar, so I came in. Mamma said I must expect unconventionality, but really— Well, I might as well sit down. (*Sits* R. *of table, holding her bag and umbrella tightly.*) I wish mamma had taken me with her; but papa's Irish tenants won't pay any rent, so it was cheaper to have me with Mrs. Ondego-Jhones. Besides, mamma was afraid we'd meet Cousin Chauncey. He has a gold-mine, without any gold in it, out West—in Louisville, I fancy. Oh, I wish some one would come! Mamma says there is a niece, a Pawnee in petticoats, whom I am to study

up, because men like Pawnees—in petticoats.
I'm to learn American fascination in three—
(*Peals of laughter heard outside.*)

SIERRA. I hear you out there, Ted!

LADY G. Gracious, some one coming!
What did mamma tell me to say? Oh, I
know! (*Rises; comes forward smiling.*) Mrs.
Ondego-Jhones? So good of—

(*Pillow flies in* R. E., *lands at her feet.* SIER-
RA *follows it; stands aghast, staring at*
LADY G. *Cushion flies in* L. E., *followed by*
TED, *who is equally amazed.* LADY G. *drops
bag and umbrella, turns in wonder from one
to the other.*)

SIERRA. Oh, pray excuse us! We're having a little lark. Don't be frightened.

TED. Yes, that's all. No cause for alarm.

LADY G. (*frigidly*). Thanks. (*To* SIERRA.)
Is Mrs. Ondego-Jhones at home?

SIERRA. No, not at present. Lady Guinevere Llandpoore, I presume. Let me present myself—Miss Bengaline, Mrs. Ondego-
Jhones's niece.

LADY G. Charmed to meet you, Miss Bengaline. (*Aside.*) The fascinating Pawnee.

2

(*Brings* SIERRA *down front.*)   Please present
me to that young gentleman.   He spoke to
me, and I can't answer until we are introduced.   (*Goes back,* C. ; *stands with her head
carefully averted from* TED.)

SIERRA (*aside*). Now, if I tell her his name,
she'll tell aunt.   What shall I do?   (*Goes to*
LADY G.)   It's not customary over here, Lady
Guinevere, to—er—to—

LADY G. To what?   (*Looks at* TED.)   Oh!
I didn't notice his clothes before.   He is the
butler—

SIERRA (*interrupting*). That's the idea.
And, as I say, it's not customary ; but, to
oblige you, I will present Larkins, my aunt's
new butler, to you.

LADY G. (*sinking into a chair*). Introduced
to a butler !   What would mamma say ?

TED (*amazed*). What is that ? Come, I say—

SIERRA (*shaking her fist behind* LADY G.).
'Ssh !   Do you, or do you not—er—buttle—
for Mrs. Ondego-Jhones ?

TED. Eh ! Oh ! (*Laughing.*) I do, mum.

SIERRA (*sternly*). Very good.   Then carry
Lady Guinevere's luggage to her room.   The
second story front.

TED. Yes, mum. (*Picks up mackintosh, etc., goes towards door,* c.)

LADY G. Stop a bit. Mamma said I was to give my brasses to—er—somebody, and have my boxes brought here.

SIERRA. Larkins, take Lady Guinevere's *brasses*, and telephone for a messenger to see after her *boxes*. (TED *bows; comes back; takes checks.*)

LADY G. (*timidly*). Stop a bit. (*Takes out purse; gives* TED *a piece of silver.* SIERRA *laughs.*)

TED. Thank you, your ladyship. (*Aside.*) Confound her impudence! (*Exit* c.)

LADY G. Miss Bengaline, is it possible that nice young man is a common butler?

SIERRA. Frankly, Lady Guinevere, he is a most uncommon one. His life is a perfect romance.

LADY G. How lovely! Tell it me. (*Aside.*) Now I'll *study* her.

SIERRA. All right. (*Aside.*) Isn't she prim? I'll take a rise out of her. (*Sits on sofa.*) First, you must know, he is the son of rich parents, who brought him up in the lap of luxury, sent him to Harvard, and then—er—

LADY G. (*drawing her chair nearer*). Died?

SIERRA. Thanks. Died when he was a mere infant.

LADY G. But I don't understand. Is Harvard a kindergarten?

SIERRA. Technically, no; but I mean a *legal* infant of twenty years; so he required a guardian, who in the basest way—er—er—

LADY G. Absconded? All Americans do.

SIERRA. Well, he didn't. He put all the money in an English swindle—an Orange Pekoe Trust, which went up the flume. (*Points up.*)

LADY G. Went where? (*Looks up.*)

SIERRA. Up the flume—burst, smashed, crashed (*very fast*). So Ted—Larkins was ruined, and was opening oysters in a Bowery saloon, when aunt found him and brought him here. How does that strike you?

LADY G. It's beastly jolly—I mean highly entertaining. Now I understand the pillow fight. I must tell your aunt.

SIERRA (*springing up*). Oh, don't! Please don't.

LADY G. Why not? I admire her noble

work of charity. At home he'd only have received out-door relief or soup tickets.

SIERRA. But this is such a delicate case, Lady Guinevere, and my aunt is *so* modest about her charities. The least allusion would— You understand? (*Aside.*) Six fibs since breakfast. Oh, Sapphira!

LADY G. (*rising, goes to the table; sits*). If you think she'd be displeased, count on my silence.

SIERRA. Displeased is a mild word. Besides, aunt thinks pillow-fighting is hoydenish. (*Hunts under all the chairs for her chewing-gum, talking all the while.*) You see, papa sent me East to be toned down, and aunt is doing her best; but there's too much raw material in me to make a good society girl, and that's a fact. (*Finds gum, puts it in her mouth, sits on sofa, with her feet up.*)

LADY G. (*aside*). How easy she is! I wish I could do that. I'll ask her to teach me. (*To* SIERRA, *timidly.*) Miss Bengaline, I've a favor to ask. Don't think it strange, but will you teach me a little slang and fascination?

SIERRA (*demurely*). Mixed or separate?

LADY G. (*earnestly*). I fancy they always go together, for my brother Clarence says the American girls are perfectly fascinating, because you never can tell what they will do or say next. He says they are more fun than a box of monkeys!

SIERRA. Indeed. He's very *kind*. (*Aside.*) A box of monkeys!

LADY G. (*seriously*). Oh, Clarence knows! So I thought if you'd kindly teach me a little, I might be more of a success when I go back.

SIERRA (*jumping up*). I'll do my best. Of course fascination isn't like acting. You can't learn it in six lessons. But if you will teach me English repose, I'll give you a little American dash. (*Aside.*) When I've finished, "a box of monkeys" won't be a circumstance to her.

LADY G. Then it's a bargain. Shall we begin now?

SIERRA. Oh no; wait till after lunch, when you are rested. Let me show you to your room. Now, then, Lady Guinevere, hook on.

LADY G. Do what? And please call me Guinevere.

SIERRA. All right. Call me Sierra. (*Puts*

her arm around LADY G.) That's hooking on. And now we'll make tracks for your room.

LADY G. (*triumphantly*). I've hooked on, and I'm making tracks.

(GIRLS *exeunt* R. *Bell rings violently several times. Enter* CHAUNCEY OGLETHORPE. *He looks about dubiously.*)

CHAUNCEY. Ahem! Any one at home? (*Looks all around; listens; smiles.*) What a lucky thing! I'll have a bit of time to prepare my speech to Mrs. Ondego-Jhones and conquer my beastly bashfulness. (*Comes forward.*) Queer house! Quite a paradise for tramps. Front door hospitably open; no one in sight. (*Sits by table; takes out letter.*) Mrs. Campell's note of introduction. Wish I deserved half she says of me. Now, if I'm only not overtaken by an attack of shyness, all will go well. Very neat scheme. My revered aunt writes to know if I remain on my ranch all winter. I see the trap, reply, "Certainly; my partner is East, and I have to stay by our gold-mine." Invite her to visit me. She then feels confident that Guinevere is secure from my attentions, and leaves

her here.   The day her ladyship starts West
I arrive here, present myself to Guinevere's
hostess, make a favorable impression, make
desperate love to Guinevere all winter, and
when my aunt returns she will find her im-
pecunious nephew established as her son-in-
law elect.   Lovely prospect! (*Rises; walks
up, and down.*)   Bah! desperate love, I say.
Don't I know that the minute a female appears I shall become a tongue-tied, stuttering
idiot?   I always do.   What is there in a petticoat that induces total suspension of all my
faculties?   Then, again, how can I stay here
all winter?   Ralston thinks I'm in California,
keeping my eye on that gold-mine, minus the
gold.   I've a good notion to go back.   The
idea of meeting two strange females and
Guinevere, and explaining things! Gad! it
makes me burn all over. (*Lays letter on table,*
R. C.; *takes off his top-coat; hangs it on chair,*
R.)   Jove! I'll step into this side-room, and
collect my senses. (*Exit* L.)

TED (*enters* R.; *sees coat and hat.*) That's a
give-away.   I'll remove that circumstantial
evidence of my presence, and then write to
Sierra. (*Catches up wraps; throws through*

R. ; *exit ; comes back ; sits down by table.*)
Now for my note. What will I write on?
(*Sees letter left by* CHAUNCEY.) Ah! this
will do—an old invitation. (*Tears off blank
side ; throws other under table ; writes.*)
" Dearest Sierra,—I can't keep up this idiotic
deception any longer. Will not wait to see
your aunt. Will keep my eye out for the
red book. Can't you—" (*Looks up.*) Jove!
some one coming. I'll go in the library.

(*Rushes off*, R. *Enter* CHAUNCEY, L.)

CHAUNCEY. I've got my speech on the tip
of my tongue. It's rather neat, too. (*Comes
forward, smiling.*) Ah! Mrs. Ondego-Jhones,
I presume. Allow me—

(SIERRA *enters*, C. *He looks at her in horror;
retreats backward to sofa, where he involun-
tarily sits down, still staring.*)

SIERRA. A strange man in a petrified condition. Who is he, and what petrified him?
Oh, I see! It's the butler from Mrs. Campell. Well, he sha'n't stay and interfere with
Ted. (*To* CHAUNCEY, *haughtily.*) You've a
note from Mrs. Campell?

CHAUNCEY (*rising; looks at floor.*) Yes.
Mrs. Ondego - Jhones— I— Oh no; too
young—I— (*Aside.*) Confound it!

SIERRA. I am Miss Bengaline; but my
aunt left full instructions in regard to you.
(*Aside.*) She said ask the usual questions.
What *are* the usual questions? Oh, I know!
(*Sits by the table.*) Are you sober?

CHAUNCEY (*coming down front*). She thinks
I am intoxicated. I must explain. I'll make
a bold effort. (*Turns suddenly to* SIERRA.)
I'm as sober as you are.

SIERRA (*springing up*). What? How dare
you address me so impertinently? That settles it. My aunt would never engage you. I
will bid you good-morning, and advise you
to remember that the first requisite in a butler is a respectful manner. (*Walks back to
window.*)

CHAUNCEY. Butler? I? Oh, madam! there
—is—a—mistake— I—er—I— (*Aside.*) I
give up. (*Crosses* R.; *stands looking down,
twisting his chain.*)

SIERRA (*coming down* L. *front*). He's a lunatic.
He can't meet my eye; can't keep his hands
still; talks wildly. I must humor him. (*To

CHAUNCEY.) Some mistake you say. Didn't you come from Mrs. Campell?

CHAUNCEY (*aside*). The room is going around, and my tongue thickening. (*To* SIERRA.) Yes; I've a letter—a—a—letter, you know—a—you know— (*Aside.*) She thinks I'm a fool.

SIERRA. Poor fellow! He's very nice-looking. (*To* CHAUNCEY.) Allow me to see your letter.

CHAUNCEY (*rushes to table, stumbling over a chair; hunts for letter*). Jove! it's gone!

SIERRA. The letter?

CHAUNCEY. Yes. Good-morning. Er— I'll call again—I'm far from well— I'm—er—er—feverish— Jove! my hat and coat are gone!

SIERRA. I'm horribly frightened.

CHAUNCEY (*coming down* R. *front. Aside*). What must she think? I'll brace up, talk very loud and fast, and explain. (*Rushes to* SIERRA; *seizes her hand.*) Madam, I'm very shy—very shy—very, very, very shy—

SIERRA. Shy! Ted! Ted! Help!

TED (*runs in; pushes* CHAUNCEY *away*). How dare you touch this young lady? Sier-

ra, who is this fellow? (CHAUNCEY crosses R.)

SIERRA (*throws her arms about* TED). Oh,
Ted! I think he is crazy. Don't hurt him.
Don't go near him.

TED. There, my dear, compose yourself.
(*Leads her to sofa.*) Sit down, and I'll man-
age him. (*Walks fiercely up to* CHAUNCEY.)
Now, sir!

CHAUNCEY (*turning*). Sir! Why, it's Ralston! Thank fortune.

TED. Chauncey Oglethorpe! By all that's
wonderful.

CHAUNCEY. Let me explain. This horrible
tangle is the last result of my dreadful shyness. Miss Bengaline mistook me for a butler or something—I don't quite understand
what—and I tried to undeceive her, and now
she mistakes me for a lunatic.

TED. What a joke! Why are you so bash-
ful?

CHAUNCEY. I don't know. I was built that
way; increasing crescendo from a timid child
to a full-blown idiot, afraid to look a woman
in the face.

TED. Poor old chap! Never mind. I'll

settle matters. Come and be presented to Sierra. She's no end jolly. No stiffness about her.

CHAUNCEY. Oh, no! Let me sneak quietly away, and then you explain.

TED. Nonsense! (*Drags him to* SIERRA.) Sierra, let me introduce my partner, Chauncey Oglethorpe — a very much abused young man.

SIERRA (*rising*). Charmed to meet you, Mr. Oglethorpe. I've heard so much about you from Ted and your cousin Lady Guinevere that I regard you as an old friend. Pray forgive my extraordinary stupidity.

CHAUNCEY. Yes, thank you. It was stupid.

SIERRA. Now excuse me one moment, and I will tell Lady Guinevere you have arrived. (*Exit* c.)

CHAUNCEY. What a lovely girl! Has lots of tact. Don't stare a fellow out of countenance.

TED. Sierra is a trump. Have a cigarette, and be comfortable till she returns.

CHAUNCEY. Smoke here? What would Mrs. Ondego-Jhones say to that?

TED (*laughing*). She'd think it very friendly on the part of Lord Doncaster's son.

CHAUNCEY. Here goes, then. (*Lights cigarette.*) How about you? (*They sit by table.*)

TED. You don't understand. Mrs. Ondego-Jhones hasn't the pleasure of my acquaintance. I figure in her mind as a Western desperado, whom Sierra is to be separated from at all hazards. I am here clandestinely. Nice position, isn't it?

CHAUNCEY. By Jove! Ted, it's a pity she can't know you, barring impecuniosity. She'd be proud of you for a nephew-in-law.

TED. Thanks, very much. Speaking of impecuniousness, how did you leave our mine? Anything turned up?

CHAUNCEY. Yes; the men were turning up lots of dirt when I left last week, and the foreman said he thought he could manage to do the swearing for us both, so I left him, with a red and blue halo about him, watching the men work.

TED. Well, I feel sure there is gold there.

CHAUNCEY. Do you? By-the-bye, have you seen my cousin?

TED. Yes. She took me for the butler, and Sierra didn't undeceive her. Now, aside from my clothes, do you think I look like a butler?

CHAUNCEY. No; you're not sedate enough. But, by Jove, an idea. Why don't you keep up the deception? Win your way into the aunt's heart, and keep near the niece all winter.

TED (*springing up*). My dear fellow, no power on earth would induce me to place myself in such a position. Imagine me opening the door, handing the kettle, and inquiring, with a sickly grin, "Did you ring, madam?" (*Advances; meets* MRS. ONDEGO-JHONES *entering* C.; *stands in amazement.*)

MRS. O. Did I ring? I should think I did. You are — oh, I see — the butler from Mrs. Campell. Very fortunate. Please take my parcel. (*Hands him parcel;* TED *takes it silently.*)

CHAUNCEY (*rising. Aside*). What a joke! (*Crosses* L.)

MRS. O. (*advancing*). Mr. Oglethorpe, I presume. Yes. Mrs. Campell told me I should probably find you here. So pleased. Yes.

CHAUNCEY. Thanks—er—er— Will you pardon my smoking—er—

MRS. O. Don't mention it. I'm charmed to see you feel at home. Now, before we go any further, which is your hotel?

CHAUNCEY. The—er—St. James.

MRS. O. Very good. My man shall go right down and order your luggage sent here ; for my house must be your home while you are in the city. As I said to Mrs. Campell, Lord Doncaster's son has every claim on my hospitality. Excuse me one minute. (*Goes to table ; seats herself.*)

CHAUNCEY. You're very kind. (*Aside.*) She's easy enough to get on with. I wonder how she knows the governor ? (*Sits on sofa ; takes up paper.*)

MRS. O. (*to* TED). Now, my good man, we'll very soon come to an understanding.

TED (*aside*). Will we ?

MRS. O. Whatever your terms, I agree to them ; whatever stipulations you make, I agree. Having been to all the intelligence-offices unsuccessfully, I am desperate. With a houseful of company, and a reception to-morrow, I *must* have a butler. What is your name ?

TED (*muttering*). What 'll I say ?

MRS. O. Eh ? Oh ! Whuttlesay. How very peculiar ! And yet how very English. (CHAUNCEY *bursts into a fit of laughter.*)

Mrs. O. A joke, Mr. Oglethorpe?

Chauncey. Yes, er—a good joke. (*Reads.*)

Ted. Pardon me, madam, there is some misunderstanding.

Mrs. O. Eh? Oh! not Whuttlesay? What then?

Ted. Bother the name! I mean I cannot remain in your service. I'm not—not—sure I could—er—suit. I haven't—buttled for several years.

Mrs. O. Buttled?

Ted. Imperfect tense—I buttle, you buttle, he buttles, or is buttled. (*Aside.*) What am I talking about?

Mrs. O. Ah! a new verb; an English revival, I presume. However, I understood you had been a valet.

Ted. A valet?

Chauncey. A valet! Jove!

Mrs. O. And it makes no difference. You are very presentable, and I must have you for to-morrow. The maids shall attend to everything else, if you will only remain, and open the door and hand the kettle. You can leave the following day; but you must stay at present.

3

Ted (*aside*). I'll do it. (*Aloud.*) Very good, madam; to oblige you, I will, on the condition that I am free to do just what I choose and nothing else.

Mrs. O. Then that is settled. (*Slips a bill into his hand.*) You'll find me practically grateful.

Ted (*aside*). My second tip.

Chauncey. He *said* no power on earth would make him do it.

Mrs. O. Whuttlesay, you may retire. Mr.—

(*Enter* Lady Guinevere *and* Sierra, c.)

Mrs. O. Ah, my dear Lady Guinevere, welcome! So very pleased to see you again. I've a pleasant surprise for you. Mr. Oglethorpe has promised me a visit.

Lady G. You are very kind to me, Mrs. Ondego-Jhones. It is indeed a delightful surprise. (*Aside.*) What would mamma say? (*Crosses* L. *to* Chauncey, *who is much embarrassed.*)

Mrs. O. Mr. Oglethorpe, permit me to present you to my niece, Miss Bengaline.

Chauncey. Thanks. We've—er—met before—

MRS. O. Indeed! Where?

SIERRA (*looking straight at* CHAUNCEY). I do not recollect meeting Mr. Oglethorpe.

CHAUNCEY (*aside*). Jove! I forgot. (*Aloud.*) Yes, I meant I had never seen anything like Miss Bengaline.

LADY G. Chauncey!

CHAUNCEY. I—er—meant I'd like to have seen—er—something like her—er—only I never had.

SIERRA. Aunt, who is the other young gentleman?

MRS. O. The other young gentleman is Whuttlesay, the new butler.

SIERRA. Whuttlesay? (*Aside.*) What a joke!

LADY G. (*to* CHAUNCEY). She said his name was Larkins.

CHAUNCEY. Hush!

MRS. O. Whuttlesay, take my wraps. (*Gives him mantle, hat, muff.*) Now, young people, follow me to prepare for dinner, and if you notice any omissions, remember my establishment is settling down after a terrific domestic cyclone.

(LADY G. *and* CHAUNCEY *exit* C. MRS. O. *and* SIERRA *follow.* SIERRA *kisses her hand to* TED, *who stands right of centre entrance. As curtain falls, he throws* MRS. O.'s *wraps violently on floor ; sinks into chair.)*

QUICK CURTAIN.

ACT II.

EVENING.

SCENE.—*The same. Enter* MRS. O., SIERRA, LADY G., CHAUNCEY, C., *in evening dress.* LADY G., *and* CHAUNCEY *come down* L., *front.*

MRS. O. Now I must leave you. I have two receptions to attend before 11 o'clock. Sierra, I leave you to entertain Lady Guinevere and Mr. Oglethorpe.

SIERRA. Yes, aunt. Drive—

MRS. O. (*aside*). Do *not* say drive on. Study Lady Guinevere. Observe her air of well - bred repose, her careful language. (*Aloud.*) Lady Guinevere, you must allow

Sierra to show you my old masters. Mr. Oglethorpe, you will find my billiard-table in perfect order. Sierra, *remember! Au revoir!*

ALL. *Au revoir!* (*Exit* MRS. O., C.)

SIERRA. Do you want to see the old masters, Guinevere? They're patent Americans, you know. (*Sits* R. *of table.* CHAUNCEY *and* LADY G. *on sofa.*)

LADY G. Patent American? Old masters?

SIERRA. Yes: copies, you know. Kept up a chimney until they're sooty enough. They are all made in Nassau Street.

LADY G. How clever you Americans are!

SIERRA. Yes; we're all here. Mr. Oglethorpe, the cushions of aunt's table are as dead as Moses. She can't play a little bit. Shall we have a game?

CHAUNCEY (*looking sentimentally at* GUINEVERE). Just as you say, Miss Bengaline. But —er—why—not—simply—talk?

SIERRA. Yes; let's. I only asked because aunt suggested it.

MRS. O. (*appears* C., *in opera wrap*). I'm off, young people. Enjoy yourselves. Oh, these wretched social duties! Lady Guinevere, the rest of your trun—er—boxes have been carried to your room. Good-bye.

ALL (*rising*). Good-bye. (*Exit* MRS. O.)

SIERRA. Oh, Guinevere, do let me help you unpack your "trunk boxes," and show me your London gowns. Mr. Oglethorpe, will you excuse us a few minutes?

CHAUNCEY. With pleasure.

LADY G. Chauncey!

CHAUNCEY. Well, I—er—didn't mean—

SIERRA. We can imagine what you meant. Let me assuage your grief with papers—English, French, American. (*Lays papers on table.*) Now have a cigarette, and make yourself at home till we return. (GIRLS *exeunt* C.)

CHAUNCEY. A very nice little girl. She knows what a fellow likes after dinner—solitude, smoke, and news. (*Lights cigarette. Sits* R. *of table.*)

(*Enter* TED *cautiously*, L.)

TED. Is the missus off?

CHAUNCEY. Yes; and the girls up-stairs.

TED (*sitting* L. *of table*). Then I will have a little vacation. Well, isn't this the jolliest mix? How did you think I got on at dinner?

CHAUNCEY. I was amazed at your cheek. Every time Miss Bengaline brought out that Whuttlesay with such gusto, I nearly collapsed. Indeed, between my guilty knowledge of your identity and my consummate bashfulness, I imagine Mrs. Ondego-Jhones considers me a donkey.

TED. Nonsense! All you need is confidence.

CHAUNCEY. Confidence! How am I to get it? I was born with my foot in my mouth, instead of a silver spoon. I wish you could give me a little audacity, and show me how you manage women.

TED. That's easy.

CHAUNCEY. Easy! Why, fifty times I've been on the verge of getting off a proposal to Guinevere. Led up to it neatly; really been almost coherent, you know; only to stand at the last moment gaping, with my mouth open, because she looked at me.

TED. Well, you must get more confidence, and learn diplomacy. Instead of letting her disconcert you, you must embarrass her. The way to win a woman is to—

CHAUNCEY. Yes; go on.

TED. Never let her feel certain of you; play her like a trout; tantalize her; lead her on; when she grows warm, cool off; when she comes forward, retreat. Be fascinating, but a little out of her reach. When she is wrought up to the proper point, propose, and she's yours.

CHAUNCEY. Is that how you won Miss Bengaline?

TED (*meditatively*). Well, no. But it's the way she won me, and it is a splendid theory. Poor rule that won't work both ways, you know.

CHAUNCEY. Do you fancy I could do that kind of thing?

TED. Certainly. All you need is a little practice to give you confidence. I'll show you. Courtship made easy. Here. (*Pins afghan about his waist; sits on sofa, fanning himself with newspaper.*) Now, then, I'm a perfect lady. Imagine me Lady Guinevere, and propose to me.

CHAUNCEY (*goes to the door*). Now watch me lead up to my point gracefully. (*Comes forward.*) Good - evening, Guinevere. I've been waiting two years to say something.

TED (*coquettishly*). Oh, Chauncey!

CHAUNCEY. Well, I have. I love you; be my wife.

TED. Is that your idea of "leading up to it?" You'd frighten her into saying no. Allow me. (*Pins afghan on* CHAUNCEY.) Now, then, let me show you my ideas. (CHAUNCEY *sits on sofa.* TED *crosses* R. *Coming forward.*) Ah, Guinevere, how fortunate to find you alone! Thought I'd drop in a moment on my way to the A's and B's and C's. Horrid grind, society! That will give her the idea you are much sought after, and the instant a girl thinks you a social exotic, she wants you.

CHAUNCEY. I see. Now I'm Guinevere. Can't you make it two minutes, or do you think time spent with a cousin is wasted? (*Fans himself, looks at* TED *coquettishly.*)

TED (*sentimentally*). Time spent with you, Guinevere, goes all too fast. Are you going to the curling match? After a compliment, put on the brake with a commonplace remark. That whets the feminine appetite.

CHAUNCEY. I see; caviare, as it were. Where were we? Oh, I recollect! I'm afraid you are a sad flatterer.

TED. Truth cannot flatter. That's old, but

invaluable. (*Takes* CHAUNCEY's *hand.*) What an exquisite bangle! Turkish, is it not? May I examine it?

CHAUNCEY. It's wished on.

TED (*sitting beside* CHAUNCEY *on sofa*). Wished on? By whom?

CHAUNCEY (*shyly*). My mamma.

TED. Oh, that's all right. Dear little hand!

CHAUNCEY. Oh, you needn't hold my hand. Mamma wouldn't like it.

TED. Give me the right to.

CHAUNCEY (*with great artlessness*). How?

TED (*putting arm around* CHAUNCEY). Give me yourself. Then your hand is my hand, and a man has a perfect right to hold his own hand. That's logic.

CHAUNCEY. Logic? It's impudence.

TED. Same thing. You love me, darling, don't you. Say that as a matter of course. Women like the masterful style of wooing.

CHAUNCEY (*laughing*). Do you love *me?*

TED (*laughing*). I adore you. (*Kisses* CHAUNCEY.) Is it yes?

CHAUNCEY. Ask mamma. (*Jumps up.*) Jove! I wish Guinevere were here now! I'd just fire off my proposal like a ton of brick.

Ted. New way of making a mash, eh? Well, good-luck to you, old fellow, when you do meet her. Why don't you do it to-morrow evening? Ask her to waltz; then get her into the conservatory. There's everything in the surroundings.

Chauncey. I'll do it. Say, Ted, if it's not too much of a bore, show me how to "back" my partner without tearing her dress to ribbons, and make her my enemy for life.

Ted. All right.

(*Whistles waltz. They dance round the stage,* Chauncey *tripping over afghan.* Girls *heard laughing.*)

Ted. The girls! Your cousin mustn't find me here.

(*Exeunt* Chauncey *and* Ted, r. *Enter* Girls, c.)

Lady G. (*timidly*). Rats!

Sierra. Guinevere, the modest, shrinking air with which you sling slang is simply convulsing.

Lady G. I know I don't—er—sling it very well yet, but I mean to learn. Mamma says it's time we girls rallied around our young peers, and saved the honor of old England. Do you know, Sierra (*tragically*), there's hardly a marriageable duke left. All snapped up by the Americans; and now they're commencing on our rich commoners.

SIERRA. How greedy! (*Sits on table; swings her feet.*) We get there every time, though.

LADY G. (*aside*). How fascinating. (*To* SIERRA.) Let me do that too. (*Sits by* SIERRA *on table, imitating every motion.*) *Do please* teach me fascination.

SIERRA (*aside*). Now for a circus. (*Aloud.*) It's very hard to be fascinating in cold blood with a female, but I'll do my best, because I cottoned to you from the first. Sabe?

LADY G. (*timidly*). I'm on to your lead. Is that right?

SIERRA. You're getting on like a house afire. (*Aside.*) How pleased her brother will be!

LADY G. Thanks, dear. But there's something wrong yet. When I told your aunt her cook wasn't any slouch, she seemed really thunder-struck. Yet Clarence told me that *slouch* was a common American expression.

SIERRA. It is. About as *common* as a word can be. You're right there. How I would like to meet your brother! As I cannot, suppose you play his part, and I'll entertain you in real American style, so you can see the true inwardness of our resemblance to a box of monkeys. (*Goes off*, c.)

LADY G. How charming she is! But I'm learning. (*Enter* SIERRA.) Good - evening, Miss Bengaline.

SIERRA (*in door-way*). " Well, this is way up!" That's New York. (*Coming forward*). "Shake, old chap," is Chicago, and "Put it there, pard," is Boston. (*Shakes* GUINEVERE'S *hand violently*.) Local dialects, you know.

LADY G. (*laughing*). Oh, how funny! Do you girls really say such things? (*Sits on sofa*.)

SIERRA. Please remember you are your brother.

LADY G. What would he say?

SIERRA. He would probably stick his monocle in his eye, look as though he was trying

to recollect an idea left him by his grand-
father, and say — nothing, unless he could
manage some nice little compact repartee,
such as " Gad !" or " Moses !"

LADY G. Yes, I fancy Clarence would say
" Moses !"

SIERRA. Of course. Ever so many English-
men come to papa's ranch. I know their
style.

LADY G. Well, I'll be Clarence again. Moses! Did you ever hear—oh! Thingummy
—you know the opera that German beggar
wrote, three old ladies playing with a clothes-
line, three fates, or something, by—Wagner.
Do you like that sort of thing?

SIERRA. You've got that down fine. Now
watch, Guinevere, I'm going to let monkey
No. 1 out of the box. (*Jumps up.*) Like
Wagner! Never while there's a cat left to
our back fence. I like tunes with dances in
between each verse. But above all dances—
Say, I'll dance you a breakdown so you can
see how I entertain young men.

LADY G. Oh! yes, do!

(*Dances break-down or fancy dance; throws herself into a chair* R. *of table.*)

SIERRA. There! A tune like that snatches Wagner bald-headed.

LADY G. Jove! Is that right?

SIERRA. Correct. Now, then, Guinevere, I'll let monkey No. 2 out of the box. Waltz up, and I'll show you how to play poker. (LADY G. *waltzes stiffly to table.*)

SIERRA (*laughing*). Waltz up is slang, my dear. A charming Americanism for approach.

LADY G. (*sits opposite* SIERRA). Oh! Then let me write it down. (*Takes out tablets; writes.*) "Snatch Wagner bald-headed. Waltz up." I've quite a nice little list.

· SIERRA (*dealing cards. Aside*). I haven't the faintest idea of how poker is played, and my imagination is nearly exhausted. (*To* GUINEVERE.) We each have eleven cards, match all we can, and put our money on the —er—pot.

LADY G. Where is the pot?

SIERRA. The pot? Oh, that's a term derived from potluck, meaning that you plank your pile on whatever happens along. Plank your pile means invest your funds.

LADY G. I see—at least I'm on to the game! I got that off nicely, didn't I?

Sierra. Yes: you're as bright as a red wagon.

Lady G. Thanks, dear. Are your feet crossed? (*Looks under table.*)

Sierra (*crossing her feet*). Certainly. American girls *always* cross their feet, plant one hand on their hip thus (*suits action to word*), talk at the top of their nasal voices, contradict their elders, say "I guess," and laugh incessantly. That is the groundwork of the fascination which makes them (*sarcastically*) more fun than a box of monkeys.

Lady G. (*imitates* Sierra's *pose. Takes up tablets; reads*). Now for the game, ante up, and watch me snake the pot.

Sierra (*laughing*). Good!

Lady G. Oh, I'm learning. _(*Consults tablets; throws pair of kings on table.*) Get on to those, and fork over the boodle.

Sierra. What? Guinevere, where *did* you get those—those expressions?

Lady G. Out of an English novel called *The Western Belle; A Prairie Romance.* The heroine in it talks that way. Isn't it right?

Sierra. Right? Oh, certainly, beautiful!

How pleased your brother will be with your progress!

LADY G. (*innocently*). Yes. Won't he?

SIERRA. Undoubtedly. Suppose we don't play any more poker. I will teach you that gem of a song. (*Rises; comes down front.*) My pupil is so far ahead. I shall have to retire.

LADY G. (*joining her*). Yes; do teach me the song.

(*They put arms about each other; dance.* TED *and* CHAUNCEY *enter; stop in amazement,* R.)

CHAUNCEY. My proper cousin!

TED. Sierra dancing a break-down! (GIRLS *stop,* L.)

LADY G. Chauncey with the romantic butler!

TED (*crossing to* SIERRA). Sierra, what are you up to? (*They retire up to window.*)

LADY G. (*crossing to* CHAUNCEY). The butler called her Sierra. Did you hear?

CHAUNCEY. Hush! He isn't a butler.

LADY G. No? Who is he?

CHAUNCEY. My partner, Edward Ralston, disguised. The aunt don't know him.

4

LADY G. How romantic !

SIERRA (*coming forward with* TED). Guinevere, Mr. Ralston desires to be presented to you in his proper character. (TED *bows.*)

LADY G. (*timidly holding out her hand.*) Shake, old chap.

TED. Pardon ?

LADY G. (*confused*). I mean, put it there, pard.

TED (*amazed*). Certainly. (*Shakes hands.*)

SIERRA. Ted, I want you one moment. (*They retire to piano.* SIERRA *sits down, playing softly while* TED *talks to her.*)

CHAUNCEY. Guinevere, it's not my affair, you know, but where did you pick up those dreadful words ?

LADY G. They are not dreadful. Mamma said I was to acquire a little American fascination, so I could captivate a duke.

CHAUNCEY. Do you want to captivate a duke ?

LADY G. No ; but I must obey mamma.

CHAUNCEY. Only till you — er — marry. Look here, Guinevere—look here—(*tying his handkerchief into knots*)—I—I—want to—to tell you something.

LADY G. Yes, Chauncey.

CHAUNCEY (*desperately*). I'm — I — I love you. I know you think I'm a stammering idiot. I know you won't have me. I don't wonder. I wouldn't were I you. I'm shy and poor, my gold-mine won't pan out, and oh, Guinevere, say it quickly!

LADY G. Say what?

CHAUNCEY. No.

LADY G. (*shyly*). I'd much rather say yes.

CHAUNCEY. You dear lovely girl! (*Kisses her.*)

LADY G. Chauncey! Think of Sierra and Mr. Ralston!

CHAUNCEY. Oh, they're engaged themselves. Miss Bengaline, Ed, congratulate me. Guinevere accepts me.

SIERRA (*coming forward*). I do congratulate you both.

TED. And I. (*Brings* CHAUNCEY *down front.*) Did you try my receipt?

CHAUNCEY. No. I shut my eyes, and dived in, and Guinevere landed me.

SIERRA. Young people, I propose a grand celebration of this happy event. What shall it be — music, dancing, charades?

LADY G. Charades; and Chauncey and I will be audience. (*Sits on sofa;* CHAUNCEY *follows.*)

SIERRA. Very good. Come, Ted. (*To* TED.) It's the only kindness we can show them, to leave them alone. (*Exit* TED *and* SIERRA, R.)

CHAUNCEY. Guinevere, I'm the happiest fellow alive. What a relief to have the proposal over!

LADY G. (*innocently*). Yes; isn't it?

CHAUNCEY (*taking her hand*). Dear little hand. (*Bell rings.*)

LADY G. They're ready. Let go my hand.

TED (*entering* R.). Lady and dear old chap, you are now invited to witness a performance unequalled in the annals of the stage. Two artists, unassisted by scenery, will act out a word of four syllables in one scene, which requires twenty-four characters, a chorus, a village green, a raging ocean, and a bloodhound. (*Bows. Exit* R.)

CHAUNCEY. Jove! how he rattles on! I wish I was clever.

LADY G. You are clever, Chauncey. I

don't like men who are so awfully talkative.

SIERRA (*from door*). Ready?

LADY G. Let her go (*consults tablets*), Gallagher!

TED AND SIERRA (*skip on, hand in hand; dance around stage, singing.*) We are the chorus. We are the chorus. Tra-la-la-la, tra-la-la-la. (*Stop* R. *front.*)

TED. In the absence of scenery, kindly imagine a village green surrounded by spreading oaks. In the—er—bosky shade, happy tenantry drinking air with gusto out of paper-mugs, while the oldest inhabitant, in a white smock, explains the situation to his son's wife. Is that clear?

LADY G. Yes; do go on.

TED (*in high, piping voice*). Ees, ma dear; it's a great day for me. I's ployed with t'owd squoire w'en ee were a lad, and now 'is son is a-comin' back to the old 'ouse. 'Tis a joyful day—a joyful day for I, oo is a undered and fifty-two come Lady-day. (*Weeps.*)

SIERRA. There, Father Hodge, don't ee be choildish. Sit ye in the shade, hand 'ave a mug o' beer. Young squoire, ee won't forgit ye. Ee'll be 'ere directly with his sweet-'art, Lady Clare, and 'is wicked cousin. A bad lot, that wicked cousin — a bold, bad willian.

TED. Now we are the chorus again. (*Takes* SIERRA's *hand. Both cry together.*) Hurray! Hurray! Hurray for the young squire!

TED. Now, I'm the young squire, and Sierra is my sweetheart. (*They go back, come down smiling and bowing to imaginary chorus.*)

TED. Thanks for your hearty welcome, my honest friends. I'm rejoiced to be among you again. It's a pity my father is not alive to see this day; on the other hand, if he were, I could not decently inherit the estate. It's a poor heart that never rejoices; so enjoy yourselves. There's a roasted ox in the foreground, and unlimited beer and skittles in the background. Kindly take yourselves off, and leave me to propose to Lady Clare. (*Waves his hand. Exit chorus.*)

SIERRA. Dear Alphonse, come and sit under the shade of this noble tree, where the lime-light will reach us, and tell me about your travels.

TED (*leading her to chair*). Darling Clare,

the lime-light is full upon us, the music is softly throbbing, the time and the hour are here, and I am man enough to do my duty. I love you, darling. Will you be the young squire's bride?

SIERRA. I have always adored you.

TED. Thanks. I thought you did. I will now leave you to your inevitable soliloquy. (*Exit* R.)

SIERRA (*theatrically clasping her hands*). He loves me! Happy girl! But no, I feel a sudden thrill. Such happiness cannot last. Ah! here comes the wicked cousin. Why does he so darksomely pursue me?

(*Enter* TED, *his coat-collar turned up; high hat on.*)

TED. At last! (*Springs to* SIERRA; *grasps her by the arm.*) Listen, girl! I love you! Nay, start not! I've just murdered your uncle. Near his rigid form I dropped a handkerchief, a collar-button, an overcoat, and other articles of wearing apparel, marked with the name of my puling cousin, your lover.

SIERRA (*falling on her knees*). Cruel man! Let me fly to remove them!

TED. Not so, unless you marry me. In that case you may. Thwart me, and I accuse him before the whole village. I love you darkly, desperately, madly!

SIERRA. Oh, this is fearful! But know, proud ruffian, that not to save my darling's life would I consent to tell a lie. I defy you!

CHAUNCEY (*applauding*). Hooray! Good for you! I am the gallery, Miss Bengaline.

SIERRA. Thanks.

TED. Now all the characters are on the stage; I am still the villain. Ah! defy me? Ho, everybody! This wretch, my cousin, has murdered his benefactor in cold blood. By his victim's corpse you will find the evidence.

SIERRA. Now I faint.

TED. Yes, in my arms. And the curtain falls on a grand tableau. (SIERRA *falls into his arms.*) Now, what is the word?

MRS. O. (*enters* c.). The *word* is disgusting, atrocious!

SIERRA (*springs away from* TED). Aunt!

TED. Now for it.

MRS. O. Whuttlesay, retire. Sierra, are you crazy? Lady Guinevere, what must you think?

LADY G. I think it's lovely.

CHAUNCEY. Yes.   But what was the word?

SIERRA. Aunt, you don't understand; it was a charade.

MRS. O. (*sinking into a chair*). Charades with a butler!   Whuttlesay, leave the room.

SIERRA. Do go, Ted.

TED. No, Sierra; I will not.

MRS. O. He calls her *Sierra!*

CHAUNCEY. What a jolly row!

TED. My name is not Whuttlesay, Mrs. Ondego-Jhones, nor am I a butler.

SIERRA (*shutting her eyes*). It's coming.

TED. My name is Edward Ralston, and you must not blame Sierra.   The misapprehension arose from a perhaps not unnatural mistake on your part.

SIERRA. It's all my fault.   Don't blame Ted, aunt.

MRS. O. Edward Ralston!   How could I have been so stupid?   Sierra, you need not bristle up.   I am charmed indeed to meet Mr. Ralston.   (*Shakes* TED's *hand.*)

TED (*bewildered*). You're very good.

SIERRA. She must be delirious.

TED. You did say you were charmed to meet me?

MRS. O. Yes; and I meant it. Sierra's father has withdrawn his opposition, which was only based on pecuniary grounds, you know, and which vanish now your circumstances are altered so wonderfully.

TED. Who altered them? What are they? Oh, somebody is crazy!

SIERRA. What do you mean, aunt?

MRS. O. Is it possible? Yes; I see. Well, let me be the one to announce the news. As I went out, the postman handed me this letter (*holds up letter*) from Mr. Bengaline. Come around me, young people, and I will read it.

(CHAUNCEY *and* LADY G. *stand* L. *of* MRS. O.; TED *and* SIERRA R.)

MRS. O. (*opening letter*). "I've just sold 20,-000 head of long-horned "— No, that's not it.

ALL. Go on.

MRS. O. "The Republican triumph"—um —"present state of the tariff"—er— Ah! here it is.

ALL. Yes; do go on.

MRS. O. "The sudden find of a new lead

in the Sierra Gold-mine, owned jointly by Edward Ralston and Chauncey Oglethorpe "—

TED. Gold at last!

CHAUNCEY. Jove! it *has* panned out!

MRS. O. (*smiling*). Wait! (*Reads.*) "Has produced a state of excitement in the country which has not been equalled since '49. The superintendent has sent to San Francisco for more machinery, and telegraphed the lucky partners to come home. Speculators have already bid $600,000 for the mine. There is not an inch of ground for sale near the Sierra, and the excitement is intense."

TED. Hooray! We're millionaires! Sierra, you're my mascot!

CHAUNCEY. This will fetch your mother, Guinevere.

MRS. O. Wait! (*Reads.*) "Of course, now I will not oppose Sierra's engagement, as Ralston is a delightful young fellow." Now, my dears, isn't this a romance?

SIERRA (*kissing her*). Oh, aunt, I'm so happy.

TED. Yes, *aunt*, we're so happy! I'll run on to-night, get things in working order, return in four weeks, and then for a wedding. Eh, Sierra?

SIERRA. Oh, Ted, we mustn't be rash! We'll wait a long, long time—say *five* weeks. (*They retire up.*)

MRS. O. (*rising*). Mr. Oglethorpe, I congratulate you heartily.

CHAUNCEY. Thanks. I shall go on with Ralston, return with him, be married on the same day—

LADY G. You forget mamma.

MRS. O. My dear, your mamma can have no reasonable objection to a son-in-law worth at least half a million.

SIERRA (*coming forward*). Then you forgive us, aunt?

MRS. O. I saw through the whole thing from the first, you foolish children. Ah! you need not look incredulous. Two can play at deception.

LADY G. (*to* CHAUNCEY). What a tarradiddle! She was furious over that charade.

CHAUNCEY. I should say so. By-the-way, Ted, what was that wonderful word of yours?

TED. Why, Melodrama?

MRS. O. Melodrama? Very clever, too, if I can judge by the little I saw.

SIERRA. Yes, I thought you seemed pleased.

Mrs. O. I was.   And how very appropriate, as our little drama ends in the good old-fashioned melodramatic style—all the lovers united, everybody rich, and the hard-hearted guardian bestowing her blessing thus (*holds out her hands*), so as to make a good curtain picture.

Mrs. O., c.

Chauncey.   Lady G.   Ted.   Sierra.

QUICK CURTAIN.

THE JACK TRUST.

CHARACTERS.

LORD JACK TOWNLEY ... *The Trust, who thinks himself irresistible.*

JENNIE PATIE .... *Who quite agrees with him.*

CLORINDA DE COURCEY ..... *A humorist in petticoats.*

EULA OTIS .... *A relic of " befo' de wah."*

OLD MRS. BOOTHBY ... *Whose actions speak louder than words.*

MARIA .... *Up to snuff ! yes, ma'am ; that's what !*

THE JACK TRUST.

ACT I.

Parlor in Green Spring Hotel. Table, with register and writing materials, right centre. Large screen, right. Chairs, centre. Sofa, chairs, and table, left. Mirror, left. Pictures, etc. Entrances, centre and left.

(Curtain rises on MARIA arranging parlor.)

MARIA *(dusting and arranging furniture).* My lawsey me! "There's no fool like an old fool," and Miss Eula, she's set out ter prove it. I b'lieve if Lord Jack, he was ter say, "Here, you! black my boots!" Miss Eula, she'd take and do 'em. And all 'cause he's an English lord — jus' the same ornary sort that our grandsires fit and fought and bled and died ter get the country quit of. And it's plumb scan'alous, fur she's a good forty,

5

and he only twenty, though he orders folks roun' like he was risin' ninety. (*Strikes attitude.*) If any man was ter do me like he does Miss Eula, I'd set the door open wide, and I'd say that yeah is the openin' the carpenter made fur you-uns. Yes, ma'am; that's what!

(*Enter* Eula, L. E.)

Eula. Fo' gracious sakes! Not done yet, and the train due in ten minutes, perchance bringing a dozen guests! I declare I've nary bit of use for you in the world! You're jus' reg'lar no 'count, po' ornary white trash.

Maria. Me? Po' ornary white trash!

Eula. Yes, you. Give me the duster—though it's enough to make my po' father turn in his grave for me to do servant's work. Give me the duster!

Maria. Take it, and keep it. I'm a Virginia Picken, I am, an' your father couldn't turn no fas'er than mine in his grave if he could see me livin' out for wages. Yes, ma'am. An' before the wah the Pickens had mo' servants an' mo' horses an' mo' whiskey than the Otises ever dreamed of. Yes, ma'am; that's what! (*Flings herself on sofa; sobs.*)

EULA. Fo' gracious sakes! Quit crying, you foolish gyurl!

MARIA. You've done hurt my feelin's, an' —an'—I'm g-goin'.

EULA. Going? And the train due? Oh, Maria.

MARIA. I ain't carin' 'bout trains. I'm goin'.

EULA. Oh, Maria! (*Goes to sofa; sits beside her.*) Think of dear Lord Jack! He says no one can make his mint-juleps like you can. Think of me, mos' 'stracted with that no 'count cook in the kitchen. Of co'se I respec' your fam'ly same as my own; and if you'll only stay, I'll give you the pink silk dress I wore before the fall of Richmond. There!

MARIA (*jumping up*). The pink silk with the white lace bertha? Miss Eula, I 'cept yo'r apology. Give me the duster, an' I resume my duties.

EULA. No, no. I'll help. Jus' wipe off that window. The train might bring a score of guests.

MARIA. Yes'm, it might; but I s'pec' it won't.

EULA. Have you seen dear Lord Jack lately?

MARIA. Yes'm. He's lyin' in the hammock, drinking mint-julep and smoking cigarettes, like he always is.

EULA. Dear fellow! I s'pec' he's thinking about his book on America.

MARIA. His book on America! He 'ain't got sense enough ter write a scrap-book. Yes, ma'am ; that's what!

EULA. He has a vast and lofty intellec'—What are you staring at?

MARIA. An ole piny-woods woman in the mos' survigerous sun-bonnet I ever see.

EULA. Where's she goin' at?

MARIA. She's comin' in here.

EULA. I reckon she's selling something.

(*Enter* MRS. BOOTHBY, C. E. *She wears a gossamer circular, a sun-bonnet tied closely over her face, carries small basket on her arm. Advancing, holds out her slate to* EULA, L.)

EULA. No, I don't want any. Never use them. (MRS. B. *pokes slate at her.*) No, I tell you!

MARIA (*coming to* C.). No! she tells you.

EULA. She must be deaf.

MARIA. There's writin' on the slate.

(MRS. B. *waves slate to* EULA. *Points to writing.*)

EULA. (*takes slate—*MARIA *looks over her shoulder—reads*). "My name is Mrs. Boothby. I am deaf and dumb. I want to board here." Board here! Would you take her, Maria?

MARIA. Well, she couldn't complain much; but I'd make her pay in advance. I never heard of a piny-woods woman stopping at a hotel.

EULA. Nor I either. (*Writes.*) My terms are one dollar a day in advance.

(*Gives slate to* MRS. B. MRS. B. *takes it. Writes. Gives it back to* EULA *with a bill.*)

EULA (*reads*). "The terms suit. Here is two days in advance. I sha'n't be any trouble. All I want is to be let alone. It amuses me to watch folks; and as I can't hear what is said, or tell what I see, nobody minds old Mrs. Boothby."

MARIA. Pore ole soul! Ask her ter lay off her bonnet an' come up-stairs; I want ter see her face.

EULA. Won't you— Oh! I forgot. (*Writes.*) Won't you take off your bonnet and go to your room?

(*Gives slate to* MRS. B., *who writes; hands it back.*)

EULA (*reads*). " I never take off my bonnet on account of neuralgy in my jaw, and stairs tire my legs. I am eighty-six years old, and don't want to be bothered."

MARIA. Mighty spry ole woman for eighty-six. Writes like she was a girl.

EULA. She's got a will of her own, I reckon. But I don't want to bother her.

(MRS. B. *goes to sofa; draws up table; takes cards from her pocket; plays solitaire.*)

MARIA. Lawsey me! Watch her playin' kyards with one foot in the grave!

EULA. It's her foot, I reckon, and none of our business. Jus' set things to rights while I rub the mirror.

(*Goes to glass; looks at herself;* MARIA *dusts chairs, etc.*)

EULA. Two more gray hairs, and the crow's-feet deepening every day! Ah me! And yet, as dear Lord Jack says, is not the rich tint of autumnal beauty preferable to the glaring callowness of spring? Maria, what do you think, Lord Jack thought I was only twenty-nine!

MARIA. He mus' be a born— Has he paid his board bill yet?

EULA. His remittances have not yet arrived.

MARIA. That explains it. He's trying to use soft soap instead of hard cash.

EULA. Your levity is misplaced. His lordship has discretion. He detests gyurls, and is at this moment hiding from two bold, forward chits, who engaged themselves to him much against his will, and may at any moment arrive here.

MARIA. Crickey! Both together?

EULA. I dare say. Lord Jack met one at Marietta, and the other at Stone Mountain. And both fairly persecuted him into hiding here.

MARIA. Then how do they know where he's at?

EULA (*taking paper from her pocket*). By means of this vile paper. (*Reads.*) "Lord Jack Townley, eldest son of the Duke of

Grabshire, is drinking the waters at Green Springs.   N. B.—Rumor says his lordship is to marry one of the fairest daughters of that lovely resort very shortly."   There!

(MRS. B. *gives a hoarse chuckle; pounds table;*
MARIA *and* EULA *jump.*)

MARIA. What a queer old creature!

EULA. Never mind her.   His lordship says the instant those horrid gyurls read that paragraph they will rush here to drag him away. And he hates them—hates every woman, except—me.

(*Simpers.*   MRS. B. *chuckles again.*)

MARIA. You?   Well, I'm plumb catawumped?

EULA (*with dignity*). I am not a foolish gyurl—

MARIA. *No*, ma'am.   You're some older.

EULA. Of co'se!   And, as Lord Jack says, what is there that does not improve with age?

MARIA. He mus' be a born fool.   Why, there's shoes, an' teeth, an' hair, an' women, an' mules—

EULA. You are impertinent. His lordship says a school-gyurl is as unpalatable to a cultivated taste as this year's claret. And women, like cheese, grow mellow with age.

MARIA. He mus' be teched in his head.

EULA (*haughtily*). We will not discuss this any mo'. The names of these crude atrocities are Clorinda de Courcey and Jennie Patie. Both are, of course, young and unripe. If either of them arrives to-day, you must deny that Lord Jack is, has, or will be here. Be cautious and— (*Bell rings.*)

MARIA. Lawsey me! the train!

EULA. And Lord Jack in the gyarden asleep and unprotected. Fly to warn him, Maria, while I run to see who has come.

(*Exit* C. MARIA *exit* L., *running.* MRS. B. *goes to both entrances; looks out; comes down front; laughs. Removing bonnet and cloak, shows a young and pretty woman, handsomely dressed. Runs again to entrances. Returning, takes calico dress from basket, made very plainly, with straight skirt and full waist. Puts it on over her own gown. Business of fearing discovery. Rolls cloak* —

*up; lays it in basket; ties her sun-bon-
net closely over her face. Retires behind
screen, R.)*

(*Enter* CLORINDA DE COURCEY, *in handsome
street dress.*)

CLO. Well, I'm rattled, and running after a
man is enough to rattle any girl; that is, if
she isn't used to it. Mamma generally cor-
rals the men, and I lasso them. But here I
must act alone. (*Sits by table*, R.; *fans herself; laughs.*) What a delightful, sneaky ex-
hilaration a lark gives one! I don't wonder
men like them. When I think of mamma's
face, if she could know where I am, my spine
turns to ice; and when I think of Lord Jack
cowering under my spiked sarcasms, I'm fit
to die of laughing. How pleased he will
be, dear boy, don't yer know! He'll find he
can't offer me the devotion of a lifetime
for five weeks, and skip the morning after
I accept him, without paying the penalty.
I only accepted him to spite the other girls,
and wouldn't take him as a gift now. All
the same, during the two hours I have here
before my train goes back to Atlanta I mean

to frighten his lordship into a fit. Clorinda de Courcey isn't to be trifled with in that style. Meantime, I suppose, my dear Jack is sitting in an arbor somewhere, spooning on that fair daughter of Green Springs the paper spoke of. (*Rises ; walks about.*) This is a peculiar hotel; not a soul about. By-the-bye, I must be careful not to give my name to these people. Oh, I wish I were a man! Then I could walk boldly in and ask for Jack. But if I were a man, Jack wouldn't have proposed to me. Things are equalized very nicely, after all. Ah, here comes a girl.

(*Enter* MARIA, *out of breath,* L. E.)

MARIA. Oh! Excuse me, ma'am, but what is your name? (*Goes to table,* R.)

CLO. Clo—er—that is— What a funny question !

MARIA (*aside*). It's one of 'em. (*Aloud.*) Not at all. Guests always register on arriving. (*Opens register.*)

CLO. So they do. Well, then, my name is Norval—Mrs. Norval. (*Crosses to table,* R. ; *writes.*) Mrs. R. S. Norval.

MARIA. Where from ?

CLO. The Grampian Hills. That is (*writes*), Peoria—er—California. Is that sufficient?

MARIA (*aside*). It ain't one of 'em. (*Aloud.*) Will you go to your room now, ma'am?

CLO. My room! Well, yes. By-the-bye, are there many people here now?

MARIA. Lawsey me, no! What an idea! There's no one here now, never has been, and never will— (*Aside.*) What am I saying?

CLO. (*aside*). She's lying. (*Aloud.*) That is a peculiar statement. Come, now; there is a young man here, isn't there?

MARIA. Nary a man—at least—no, there ain't.

CLO. (*aside*). I *know* she is lying. I'll pump her. (*Aloud.*) Very good. Show me my room.

(*Exit*, C. E., *followed by* MARIA. *Mrs. B. comes from behind screen; goes to door; looks after them; exits* C. E. *Enter* JENNIE PATIE, L. E.)

JEN. (*looks timidly around*). Oh dear! No one here. How nice! (*Takes paper from her pocket; reads.*) "Lord Jack Townley, eldest

son of the Duke of Grabshire, is drinking
the waters at Green Springs." Yes, it is the
place, and I suppose Jack is somewhere
about, making love to that horrid "fair
daughter" this nasty paper speaks of. I
just don't believe a word of it. Jack is very
perfidious, but it was only three weeks ago
that he ran away from Stone Mountain, the
day after he proposed to me, and he couldn't
be engaged to any one in so short a time.
Oh, dear! I wish he would happen in.

(*Enter* MARIA, C. E.)

MARIA (*aside*). I b'lieve it's one of 'em.
(*Aloud.*) Excuse me, ma'am, but what might
your name be?

JEN. It *might* be Jones, but it isn't. Why
do you ask?

MARIA. It's so you can register. (*Hands
her pen.*)

JEN. Why, let me see. (*Sits by table;
sucks pen; looking at* MARIA, *who eyes her
suspiciously.*) Oh, how funny! Who is
this **Mrs. R. S. Norval, from Peoria, California**? I never knew Peoria was there.

MARIA. Mrs. Norval. She's jus' come. I

reckon she's a play-actress. Leastways she was racing up and down like you was, when I first set eyes on her. Are you a play-actress, ma'am?

JEN. Not exactly. (*Aside.*) An excellent idea! (*Aloud.*) I'm a prima-donna.

MARIA. What's that yeah?

JEN. I sing—in opera, you know—on the stage. And my name is Capiani (*writes*)—Julietta Capiani.

(*Enter* CLORINDA, L. E.)

CLO. The girl who came on the train with me!

MARIA. Mrs. Norval, let me make you acquainted with Miss Julietta Capiani. Miss Capiani, this is Mrs. Norval, the play-actress. (*Both bow.*)

CLO. (*haughtily*). Pray who told you I was an actress?

MARIA. Lawsey me! I guessed it. Ain't you?

CLO. (*aside*). What a jolly notion! (*Aloud.*) I'm not exactly an actress; I'm a dancer—a skirt dancer. (*Sits* c.)

JEN. (*aside*). How disgusting!

MARIA. I don't see any difference. Anyway, I've got ter see after dinner. (*Exit* L.)

CLO. You have not at all the professional air, Miss Capiani.

JEN. And you're not a bit like one's idea of a dancer.

CLO. I'm not an ordinary dancer, you know.

JEN. Oh! one can see that. But don't you find it very wearing on the—er—that is—well, your ankles, you know? I read that Carmencita practised nine hours a day. Do you?

CLO. (*fanning herself*). Of course. (*Aside.*) Thanks for the hint.

JEN. (*leaning forward*). Then, except when you are asleep—deducting three hours for meals—you must dance, and kick, and stand on one toe all day.

CLO. That is the exact state of the case. You see, in a profession like mine, the muscles must be kept very, very flexible.

JEN. Fancy! Well, don't let me hinder you from practising. (*Aside.*) I'm dying to see her! (*Aloud.*) Pray go on.

CLO. Thanks; I will. (*Rising; comes down* L. F. *Aside.*) I've been just a trifle too clever. Why didn't I say I was a book agent? However, here goes! (*Dances military schottische, talking over her shoulder.*) Your work, in its way, is as arduous as mine, is it not, Miss Capiani?

JEN. Just about; scales from morning to night.

CLO. Then pray don't let me interrupt.

JEN. You are very kind, Mrs. Norval. (*Clears her throat. Aside.*) How can I sing? (*Aloud.*) How exquisitely you dance! I never saw such grace, such ease. But you don't kick.

CLO. (*aside*). Me kick! (*Aloud.*) Consider my costume. I *never* kick except in my room or on the stage, where kicks must be had.

JEN. So I've observed.

CLO. But you are not singing.

JEN. (*nervously*). Please don't judge my voice by this specimen. I've a bad sore throat.

CLO. And a doctor's certificate in your pocket, of course; they all do.

JEN. Certainly.

(*Sings and acts out,* "When love is young," *etc.*)

CLO. I'm almost dead!

(*Drops into chair,* R., *fans herself, and watches*
JENNIE.)

JEN. (*coughs violently at end of verse, falls
into chair,* R. C.). This is awful!

(*Enter* EULA *and* MARIA, L. E.)

MARIA. Ladies, Miss Eula Otis, who keeps
the hotel. Miss Eula, this is Mrs. Norval, the
dancer, and Miss Capiani, the singer. (*All
bow.*) There! Now you know each other.

EULA. Very happy to meet you, ladies.
Of course I've heard of you both favorably
through the press, but since the wah I go but
little to gayeties of any kind. I assure you,
therefore, it is doubly gratifying to welcome
you here.

CLO. You are very kind, Miss Otis. (*Aside.*)
What a fib!

JEN. I didn't know my fame had spread so
far. (*Aside.*) She's a humbug!

MARIA. Dinner is ready, ladies. Jus' step
out this way. (*Exit* C. E.)

BOTH GIRLS. Thanks. (*Exit* C. E.)

EULA (*soliloquizing*). They're just two crude
gyurls—pink and white and silly. Specially

6

the married one; she's as undignified as the other.

(Enter MARIA, C.*)*

MARIA. Lawsey me! Miss Eula, watch you standing here, an' the new women waiting for their dinner, an' Lord Jack a-clamoring for his; an' ole Mrs. Boothby, she's jus' handed me a note on her slate, ter say she wa'n't a-goin' ter eat along of the folkses, but mus' have her dinner in the parlor—leastwise a cup of tea an' some toast; an' here's a note for you from Lord Jack. *(Exit* C.*)*

EULA. Dear boy! Where are my glasses? Ah! here.

(Puts on eye-glasses; reads aloud.)

"Get those two girls out of the house at once. I saw them through the balusters when they went to dinner. They are dangerous. Devotedly yours, Jack."

(Enter old MRS. B., L. C.; *sits on sofa,* L.; *draws up table; plays solitaire.)*

EULA. Good heavens! What a situation! Dangerous, how? I must see his lordship at once. *(Exit* C.*)*

(*Enter* CLORINDA, L. *Walks about, looking on floor.*)

CLO. Where can I have dropped it? I should hardly care to have to telegraph to mamma for the money to get home with, especially as Jack is not here. What could that paper have meant by such a farrago of lies? Ah! here's my purse. (*Picks it up; sees* MRS. B.) Gracious! What a figure of fun! Another relic of "befo' the wah," I suppose. But I am losing my dinner.

(*Walks suddenly to* C. D.; *runs into* MARIA, *entering with large tray. Both exclaim; come down front.*)

MARIA. My lawsey me, Mrs. Norval! You nearly made me spill Lord—that is—this yeah dinner!

CLO. I thought you said there were no other guests in the house?

MARIA. There ain't.

CLO. Then who is this for? The family skeleton?

MARIA. Crickey! It's for—for ole Mrs. Boothby.

CLO. Is that she? (*Points to sofa.*)

MARIA (*looking over shoulder*). Yes, ma'am.
She's eighty-six years ole, deaf and dumb,
hasn't nary tooth in her jaw, an' always
wears her bonnet 'cause she has neuralgy.
Mightily entertaining ole lady. Yes, ma'am;
that's what!

CLO. (*pensively, looking at tray*). Um! Not
a tooth in her head, and yet fried chicken, let-
tuce, corn pone, claret, cheese, and pie. Maria, some one has told a lie.

MARIA. You've got me catawumpussed, but
I 'ain't told nary lie.

CLO. (*sweetly*). Then give the dear old lady
her dinner, Maria.

MARIA (*banging tray down on* MRS. B.'s *table*). There!

(MRS. B. *rises, throws tray on floor; sits;
goes on playing solitaire.*)

CLO. Oh, Maria! you might as well own
up. Who is that dinner for? (*Laughs.*)

MARIA. I never did see such a curious creature. (*Kneels on floor, picking up dishes.*)
Why can't you mind your own business?
Drat the old thing! Who'd have supposed
she had such a temper?

(*Enter* EULA, C.; *stands amazed.*)

EULA. What is all this? The dinner on the floor, Mrs. Norval laughing, and Maria scolding! Maria, what *is* all this? Speak! I insist!

MARIA. Hush!

(*Points to ceiling, then to tray; puts finger on her lips; shakes her head at* CLORINDA.)

EULA. Oh! I'll soon settle her. Maria, go and see if the train is on time.

MARIA. Yes, ma'am. (*Exit*, L., *carrying tray.*)

EULA (*advancing to* CLORINDA, R. C.). Mrs. Norval, I regret to say I cannot accommodate you overnight.

CLO. Indeed! Why not?

EULA. Because I—I— Well, I don't want any stage-players in my house.

(*Enter* JENNIE, C.)

CLO. Then your objection applies to Miss Capiani?

EULA. Certainly.

JEN. (*crossing to* CLORINDA, R. C.). What is the matter?

EULA. I object to having such as you in my nice quiet little hotel, and you *can't* stay. (*Crosses to* L.; *stands by* MRS. B.)

CLO. You're an impertinent old cat, and I'm going as soon as the train comes.

JEN. So am I. (*Aside.*) What would mamma say?

EULA. Befo' the wah my pa was the proudest man in nine counties, and as his daughter, you are beneath my notice. The train is due in ten minutes.

MARIA (*running in*, L.). Oh, Miss Eula! Oh, my! Lawsey me! A construction train has done jumped the track at Nickajack Junction, and all trains both ways have done quit running till to-morrow. Yes, ma'am; that's what!

CLO. No train! That knocks me out.

JEN. No train! What will mamma say?

EULA. Then you'll have to stay. Oh, dear!

(LORD JACK *runs in, laughing*, C.)

JACK. Well, you got them off. (*Sees girls.*) Oh, good Gad! the girls! (*Stands aghast.*)

JEN. AND CLO. Jack!

Tableau.

Mrs. B.

Maria.   Jack.   Jennie.

Eula.   Clorinda.

QUICK CURTAIN.

ACT II.

(*Enter* Maria, c. d.)

Maria. Well, talk about your dime novels! If any one of 'em can get ahead of the doings in this yeah house, I'd like to see 'em. Here's Miss Eula cracked over Lord Jack and 'stracted with jealousy of them two play-actresses, an' them jealous of each other, an' Lord Jack dodgin' of all, an' ole Mrs. Boothby tagging roun' and peeping and prying, like she was a revenue raider after a " blind tiger." An' me —lawsey me! I sides with 'em all. Yes, ma'am; that's what!

(Clorinda *dances in*, l. d.)

Clo. (*sinking into chair*, r.). Only you, Maria? What a relief! Do you know, Maria, you are a very pretty girl?

MARIA. Me? Crickey! What an idea! What does you-uns want me ter do, Mrs. Norval?

CLO. Oh, not much. Just to help me out in a little joke. You see, I—er—in fact— well, I want to see Lord Jack alone for a moment, and he doesn't at all want to see me. As a matter of fact, I fancy you are the only woman in the house he dares face.

MARIA. Yes'm, that's so.

CLO. (*holding up coin*). Now, you see this, Maria? This is a lovely new gold dollar, and it's for you. (*Gives it her.*)

MARIA (*tying it in her handkerchief*). Oh, thank you, ma'am.

CLO. Now, Maria, there's another of those pretty things in my purse, which is yours the first time you manage to take me to Lord Jack quietly. Be discreet, and, above all, do not say a word to that cat of a Capiani girl.

MARIA. Count on me, Mrs. Norval. She's a sly-boots. Yes, ma'am; that's what! An' the way she runs after that pore dear boy is jus' awful. I'll go hunt him up now, pore lamb.

CLO. Do. Well, why don't you go?

MARIA. I 'lowed you might be goin' ter do your steps.

CLO. (*sharply*). I am not. Go at once!

MARIA. Yes'm. (*Exit* c.)

CLO. She "'lowed I might be goin' ter do my steps!" They all do. Every bumpkin in the county, having heard of "the dancin' woman over ter Miss Eula's," rides over on his mule to hang over the fence and watch me prance about the garden like a lunatic. (*Rises; walks about.*) Truly, it was clever of me to say I danced nine hours a day. Every minute I am in sight of any one I have to skip like a gazelle with a broken ankle. The chamber-maid "'lows she'd mightily like ter see me practise"—and off I go (*dances across stage, humming*), so until my room is made up. The waiter, gardener, cook, Maria, Miss Eula—all are possessed with a burning desire to see me practise. And practise I must, or own myself a humbug. (*Sinks into chair*, L.) Oh, my quivering ankles! Why didn't I say I was a book agent, or something sedentary? Meantime the train does not come, Jack dodges about, and all is gloom and mystery. Why did the Capiani cat shriek "Jack?" Why is she here? I don't believe she's a bit of a prima-donna any more than I am. Good gracious! there's that Boothby nuisance!

(MRS. B. *enters*, c.; *goes up to* CLORINDA; *gives her slate.*)

CLO. (*reading*). " Please oblige an afflicted old woman by letting her see you dance." Was there ever such a torment? (*Writes.*) With the greatest possible pleasure.

(*Gives slate to* MRS. B., *who reads; claps her hands; sits on sofa*, L.)

CLO. (*dancing jig or fancy dance, and talking*). Ugh! You old tease! The idea of making a fool of myself for you! If a train don't come soon, I'll tell the truth. Ow, I believe I've snapped a tendon! Oh! Ah!

(*Sits suddenly*, R., *by table.* MRS. B. *claps her hands; leans forward expectantly.*)

CLO. (*limps over to her, smiling sweetly*). I sha'n't dance a bit more; and you're a cheeky old idiot! So there!

(*Exit* C. MRS. B. *follows as* JENNIE *enters*, L.)

JEN. (*hoarsely*). "When love is young, all the world seems gay. Tra-la-la-la." (*Looks about.*) No one here! (*Takes out a lemon; sucks it.*) Love can be as young as it likes, but the world does *not* seem gay if it can't induce the other party to come within hailing distance. It's perfectly shameful the way Jack treats me. Me, who he swore was the only girl he had ever loved! If I am, why is Mrs. Noval here? I heard her scream "Jack!" I did. And I don't believe she's a dancer. I listened at her door this morning and there wasn't a sound. And she's so hateful. If I stop singing one instant, she's at my door with her everlasting, "Not practising, Miss Capiani? How *very* odd!" Odd! If a train does not come soon, my throat will simply crack open.

(*Enter* MARIA, C.)

MARIA. Have you seen Mrs. Norval, ma'am?

JEN. (*curtly*). No.   But I am glad to see you, Maria, for I want you to do me a great favor.   First, please accept this.   (*Gives her money.*)

MARIA. Oh, thank you, ma'am! (*Ties it in handkerchief.*)

JEN. There's as much more for you if you think you can manage to quietly come and tell me when you find Lord Jack alone.   I have a sort of—of a bet with his lordship, so he—he—

MARIA. Bless you, I understand (*winks*).   I see you running up the gyarden after him this morning.   His coat tails jus' flew out like he was—

JEN. (*hastily*). Never mind all that.   Do what you have undertaken, and, above all, do not breathe a word to that odious Mrs. Norval.

MARIA. Count on me, ma'am.   She jus' hunts that pore dear boy.   It's awful.   I wonder how she can bring herself to do it. I'll jus' go look for him now.   (*Exit.*)

JEN. (*sits by table*, R.).   What would mamma say if she could see and hear me?   Oh, dear! there comes that tiresome Miss Eula and old

Mrs. Boothby.   Now I must keep up my reputation as a self-made fool.   (*Leans head dejectedly on her hands, sings* "When love is young," *etc.*)

(*Enter* EULA *and* MRS. B.   MRS. B. *sits on sofa.*)

EULA. How exquisite !   What finish ! and what a fearful cold you seem to have, Miss Capiani !

JEN. I have.

EULA. I'm so sorry.   Mrs. Boothby just wrote on her slate to say if you didn't mind singing in her ear-trumpet for an hour or so, she'd be mightily obliged.

JEN. But I should mind exceedingly, and you may tell the old nuisance so, with my compliments.   (*Exit* C.)

EULA. There she goes after Lord Jack, I'll be bound.   I never saw such bold audacity. I must fly to warn him.   (*Exit* L.)

(MRS. B. *crosses stage ; sits at table*, R. ; *plays solitaire.*)

(*Enter* LORD JACK *and* MARIA, C.)

JACK. You are sure I am safe, Maria ?

MARIA. Of co'se. They're both lyin' down up-stairs.

JACK. Then I can sit down a minute, I suppose. (*Sits on sofa; lights cigarette.*) Any prospect of a train soon, Maria, my dear?

MARIA. I ain't none of your dears, Lord Jack, and there ain't nary prospect of a train at all. The rails is all tore up both ways. The ticket men says maybe there won't be trains for a week.

JACK. A week! If that's so, Maria, you can bet your sweet life those "tore up" rails won't be a patch to me if either of those girls finds me alone.

MARIA. Lawsey me! whatever has your lordship done to 'em?

JACK. Done! Nothing. The fact is— Sit down, Maria, and let me talk to you a bit. You're a deuced pretty girl, and look sympathetic. Can I trust you?

MARIA (*sits on sofa* R. *of* JACK). Of co'se you can. (*Winks at audience.*)

JACK. The fact is, I'm a badly used fellow. The women simply drive me mad.

MARIA. Why don't you keep away from them? (*Laughs.*)

JACK. Keep away! Come, now. I say, how can I keep away when they follow me all over the country? But we're 'way off the point. I want to appeal to your higher feelings. You have a tendency to laugh at my misfortunes.

MARIA. Me laugh! (*Winks at audience.*)

JACK. Yes, you. And it's not right. However, I'm not angry at you. Here's a dollar for you to buy some ribbon or something. (*Gives her money.*) And now I must speak seriously to you. You must understand that if either of these two girls finds me alone the consequences will be simply fearful. There! you're laughing.

MARIA. Lawsey me! I never! (*Winks at audience.*) I'm jus' full of sympathy at the way these gyurls do you.

JACK (*grasping her hand*). Listen! Isn't that the swish of a petticoat outside? Run, Maria, and see.

MARIA. Shucks! You're nervous. Let go my hand.

JACK. Let me hold it. You are my anchor —my—

MARIA (*jumping up*). I'm not your any-

thing. Idjits like you-uns can't hold prop-
erty. (*Exit, laughing.*)

JACK (*looking after her*). Cold girl! But no
matter. Thank Heaven! she is not responsive. Three responsive females in one house
are enough for any fellow. There's Eula—
poor old soul!—and Jennie, and Clorinda;
the last two are the most charming girls I
ever loved. It's all very well to say I need
not have engaged myself to them, but how
could I help it? (*Rises; comes down* F.) It
was moonlight on both occasions; I was excited on both occasions; so what more natural
than to propose on both occasions? (*Sighs.*)
Why, oh, why did they accept me? Why
should they take my moonlit maunderings
for earnest, after I had distinctly—yes, distinctly, by Jove!—expounded to them my
theory of Platonic friendship, and said I was
not a marrying man. If, after that, they
chose to take me seriously, I could only fly.
(*Walks about.*) The idea of their following!
Beastly ill-bred! Howling bad form, I call
it. I'll tell them so pretty straight too if
they do come near me. (*Sits on sofa feet up.
Sees old* MRS. B.) Ah, there's the ideal wom-

an! Can't overhear anything or answer back. Nice, inexpensive taste in dress. I really believe the poor old soul is gone on me. Everywhere I go she follows. Gad! I s'pose it's magnetism that attracts the women to me. (*Lights cigarette.*) Poor little beggars! There's Maria! I've got her on a string too — trusting little creature! (*Closes his eyes.*) Poor little girl! I must pull up.

(*Enter* MARIA *and* JENNIE, c. MARIA *points to* JACK; *tiptoes off*, c).

JACK. Is that you, Maria?

JEN. No; it's me.

JACK. Who's me? (*Opens his eyes; springs up.*) Oh! By Jove! I say—look here—you know— (*Edges to door*, L.)

JEN. (*crossing to intercept him*). You need not run away.

JACK (*devotedly*). Run from you! Jennie, how could you fancy such a thing?

JEN. How couldn't I?

JACK. Don't you know you are the only girl I ever loved? Be seated. (*Places chair* L. *of table.*)

7

JEN. (*sitting*). It's no use, Jack; I can't believe you.

JACK (*sitting on sofa, leaning across table*). Let me explain.

JEN. I shall be most happy.

JACK. Oh, Jennie, do not look at me so coldly! (*Takes her hand.*) Dear little hand! Now, my dear girl—

JEN. Let go my hand. I am not your dear girl. Don't dare to call me so.

JACK (*tenderly*). Respected miss—

JEN. (*laughing*). How absurd you are, Jack! (*Coldly.*) Let go my hand. I'm not at all amused.

JACK (*releasing her, rises; walks about*). 'Twas ever thus. I never had a dear gazelle—

JEN. I am not at all interested in your livestock. Please proceed with your explanation.

JACK (*rumpling his hair*). Well, you see, it was something after this style. From my early infancy I have been betrothed to—to—the Lady—er—Editha—er—Cheshire, a plain girl, with a Roman nose and sandy ears—I mean hair—and big ears, and all that, you know. (*Pauses.*)

JEN. Well?

JACK. Her estate adjoins ours, and so the family cooked up the match, although she had large feet, played Wagner's march from *Lohengrin* on the piano, and was a beastly tiresome girl. (*Walks about.*) Tears, protestations, all were vain.

JEN. Surely you, an Englishman, did not cry?

JACK (*wildly*). I did. Lady Editha would unnerve any one. But it was vain. I therefore fled to America; met you; loved you madly; wrote to my haughty father, imploring his consent. He wired back, "Will cut off the entail unless you leave that American girl at once."

JEN. (*rushing to him*). Oh, Jack! I see it all. Why didn't you tell me all this before?

JACK (*embracing her*). Because I hadn't made it up—my mind, I mean. I could not ask you to be a beggar's bride. (*They sit on sofa.*)

JEN. (*fondly*). Love is enough.

JACK. Yes; but money is a good thing too. And now I have glorious news. My

father's gout is moving up, and if all goes
well — that is, if physicians are in vain — I
shall be the happiest man alive, and you the
Duchess of Grabshire, in two weeks.

(MRS. B. *overturns table·with a crash; picks up
cards; goes on playing.*)

JEN. Gracious!   I didn't know she was
here.

JACK. Never mind her.   Tell me, are you
satisfied?

JEN. No!   (*Springs up; walks about.*)
Who is this creeping, crawling serpent of
a cat who dogs your footsteps?   Who is
she?

JACK. Jupiter!   What do you mean by
serpent of a cat, and all that, Jennie?

JEN. I mean Mrs. Norval, and you know
it.

JACK. Shouldn't have recognized the description, give you my word.   And if you
come to recriminations, and all that, what do
you mean by calling yourself a *prima-donna*,
and yodling around here like a—a calliope,
without a chaperon?

JEN. It's not my fault if the trains won't

run. I only expected to stop over two hours, and see you.

JACK. Exactly. It was most improper of you to come at all—so unwomanly, so beastly untrusting. Didn't I tell you you were the only girl I ever loved?

JEN. (*sitting by table*, L.). Yes; but you ran away.

JACK. Suppose I did. Or, rather, put it correctly, I withdrew my idea from your consciousness. Very good. Then was your time to show your confidence in me, and wait decently at home. Look at Evangeline. She always kept right on trusting Gabriel.

JEN. But she went after him, and she had no chaperon.

JACK. She took her cow, and even a cow is better than nothing. Besides, she was not a society girl. And I'm amazed at you—amazed, by Jove!

JEN. (*sobbing*). Oh, Jack, *please* don't scold. I'm sure I never dreamed of doing any harm, and everything is so awful. And what would mamma say?

JACK (*going to her*). Don't cry, my dear girl. And go right to your room, and—and lie down.

JEN. I'd rather stay here with you.

JACK. And I with you.   But the conventionalities! Think of your mother. As soon as you can return to Stone Mountain, I will join you, and there, under your mother's wing, we'll be as happy as the day is long.

JEN. You'll surely come?

JACK. Can you doubt me?

JEN. Jack, forgive me. (*Exit*, L., *leaning on* JACK's *arm*.)

(*Enter* MARIA, C., *laughing*. MRS. B. *lays down cards, laughs heartily*.)

MARIA. "Jack, forgive me!" An' she hadn't done a thing. Ha! ha! ha! ha! (*Sinks into chair; sees* MRS. B). Bless me! what's she cackling over? (MRS. B. *turns; sees* MARIA; *stops laughing; goes on with her game*.) I s'pose she's beat herself. Ha! ha! ha! ha!

(*Re-enter* JACK, L., *fanning himself*.)

MARIA. I shall give up.

JACK (*gloomily*). What is the joke?

MARIA (*jumping up*). Jus' a newspaper piece I was studyin' over, an' almos' died.

JACK (*sitting on chair*, C.). Indeed!   Look

here, Maria! How did Miss Patie happen to find me?

MARIA. Miss Patie? Who's she?

JACK. A slip of the tongue. I meant Miss Capiani. But no matter. I want to get up to my room, and Mrs. Norval is whisking about the hall. Go and see if the coast is clear, and no funny business this time, Maria.

MARIA. Funny business! Lawsey me! I couldn't help Miss Capiani findin' you. And you've hurt my feelin's. Yes, sir; that's what! (*Exit* c.)

JACK. A very pretty situation!—shut up with two ex-fiancées and a candidate for fiancéeship. For all I know, old Mrs. Boothby is ready to join the dance. Down that tunnel of a sun-bonnet I seem to see two dim eyes saying, "Jack, I love you." If they only knew who I was—but no, I won't even whisper it. Flirtation is the spice of life.

(*Enter* CLORINDA *suddenly*, c.)

CLO. Good-morning, my lord.

JACK (*starting back*). It can't be! It is! (*Springs to her; takes hands.*) It is my own

Clorinda!   When did you arrive, and where is Mrs. De Courcey?

Clo. *When* did I arrive?   I like that!

Jack. So do I.   It's no end jolly.

Clo. Jolly!   Well, you are a humbug. Let go my hands, Jack.   (*Goes to chair*, c.)

Jack. You never objected at Marietta; but, I see, you are fickle.

Clo. I?

Jack. No matter. If I had known you were coming I should have flown on the wings of love to greet you, Clorinda, and all that.

Clo. Were you flying on the wings of love when I so nearly caught you this morning in the garden?

Jack. You? this morning? back garden? I don't understand. I did rather hurry to escape from that odious Mrs. Norval, the dancer.

Clo. (*sarcastically*). Then you really did not know that I am Mrs. Norval?

Jack. Married?   How delightful!   And where is Mr. Norval?

Clo. It's no use pretending ignorance, Jack. I came here intending to stop over one train, annihilate you, and return to Atlanta.   Why my plan failed, you know.   It was to prevent

my name from being known that I've enacted
the ballet girl, and you must admit I've done
it well.

JACK. I jolly well like your idea. Jupiter!
To see you spinning about on your little toes
all day, and compare it with the genuine article! Ha! ha! ha!

CLO. What do you know of the genuine
article?

JACK. That's so. Why, nothing, except that
common-sense tells me they don't skip like
little hills all day.

CLO. I don't care. I showed great presence of mind.

JACK. Great! Only absence of body would
have served you better. Doubtless you've
thought of your mother's opinion of this es-
capade.

CLO. Oh yes.

JACK. And the giggles of the girls?

CLO. Certainly.

JACK. And the winks and nods and nudges?

CLO. (*calmly*). I've thought of everything.

JACK. Well, I hope it will be a lesson. In
my last letter I told you I was heart-broken
by your silence.

CLO. Did you write any letters?

JACK (*sits by her*). Stacks.   At least two letters a day.   And you never answered one.

CLO. I never received any.

JACK. Oh! this ill-regulated Southern mail!

CLO. Oh! this ill-regulated English male you mean, don't you? (*Laughs.*)   Not a bad pun for a girl, was it?   Come, try another tarradiddle; you tell them so well, so amusingly.

JACK. Amusingly!   Clorinda, you are the only girl I ever loved.   Can you doubt me?

CLO. I can, and do.

JACK (*leaning forward to gaze in her eyes*). Clorinda, look into my eyes, and tell me if I look like a man to trifle with a fond and trusting heart.

CLO. You look like a man who would flirt with his grandmother; and it will be time enough to trifle with my fond and trusting heart *when* you get it.

JACK. You said you gave it me at Marietta.

CLO. I dare say.   But I wear it on an elastic, and snapped it in again.   (*Laughs.*)

JACK (*rising*). Clorinda, it's unfair to jump

on me without hearing reason. My letters explained all, if you only had read them.

CLO. (*rising*). Why not tell me what was in them? As I said before, your tarradiddles are so amusing. Come, sit on the sofa. (*Goes to sofa with him; sits on table,* L.) Now, then, you left me in the conservatory, and flew to pack your bag— Proceed.

JACK. Well, I went to my room, and—and— I say, Clorinda, might I smoke?

CLO. Certainly.

JACK (*takes out cigarette*). Will you light it as you used at Marietta?

CLO. Certainly. (*Business of lighting cigarette.*)

JACK (*sighs; sits on sofa*). Blessed be smoking! It's typical of life too, isn't it, Clorinda? Nice things, dreams, and all that. Jolly for a bit, then only ashes!

CLO. Like your engagements, eh? But proceed. You went to your room—

JACK. Yes, I went to my room, and— I say, isn't this jolly? You and me together, with old Mrs. Boothby for chaperon.

CLO. It's simply lovely; but pray go on. You found a telegram, doubtless?

JACK. That's it. I found a telegram couched in the most mysterious terms from—from—

CLO. Ex-fiancée—girl you left behind you.

JACK. Nothing of the sort. (MRS. B. *crosses stage. Exits*, L.)

CLO. There goes our chaperon.

(EULA, *dressed exactly like* MRS. B., *enters*, C.; *goes to table*, R.; *sits down.*)

JACK. What a restless old thing she is! But, Clorinda—won't you believe me?—you are the only girl I ever loved.

CLO. Except Miss Capiani and Miss Eula.

JACK. Poor old Eula; she's a gushing old nuisance!

CLO. What an unkind way to speak of your fiancée! for Maria tells me it's all settled between you and the evergreen Eula.

JACK. Settled! I wish it were—my board bill, I mean. Until my remittances arrive, I have to keep the old lady smoothed down. As for anything else, why, she might be my grandmother.

CLO. Calm down. She's a charming antique, a flawless relic of " befo' de wah," and as such deserves a place in your collection.

JACK (*springing up*). My collection! Clorinda, why will you make game of me?

CLO. Game of you! Impossible! Even in America, where we run the wary aniseed bag to cover, and pop away at sparrows—even here we never to try to make game of— (*Pauses; gets down from table.*)

JACK. Well?

CLO. Donkeys, even if they *are* imported. (*Exit* c.).

JACK (*running to door*). Look here, I say! Jove, what a little vixen? But I like spirit in a girl. (*Comes down front; sits astride of chair, c., facing audience.*)

(MRS. B. *enters,* L. ; *sits at table,* L. ; *same pose as* EULA.)

JACK. She was all broken up. Well, I can't help it if I was born fascinating. I'm not a self-made man, so there's no conceit in saying so. It's hard on the women, but that's not my fault. (*Looks to* R.; *sees* EULA.) There's my deaf-and-dumb belle. Looks like the figure-head of a ship. (*Looks to* L.; *sees* MRS. B.) How she skips about! A minute ago she was over there. (*Looks* R.) Why, she's back. (*Looks* L.) Oh! look here, you know. I've got 'em again. (*Looks* R.) No; there are, there must be two of 'em. (*Springs up; business of looking from* R. *to* L.) Oh, this is awful! There are two. (*Backs to* C. D. *as* EULA *and* MRS. B. *advance.*)

EULA. Flight will avail you little, my lord. (*Throws off bonnet.*) In this disguise I have heard all. And now my eyes are open. I may be a gushing old nuisance, but I know my rights, and I'll trouble you to settle your account and leave my house.

JACK. Eula, my darling!

EULA. Oh yes, keep the old lady smoothed down until your remittances arrive. Back, perfidious man! (*Waves him off.* MRS. B. *imitates every gesture.*)

JACK. But, look here. Since you were here, you must have seen my fearful position between those audacious girls.

EULA. I couldn't see your face, but your voice sounded like you was enjoying yourself mightily. (*Sobs.*)

JACK (*with dignity*). Wait. (*Hands* EULA *to chair,* L. MRS. B., R., *stands between them.*)

JACK. Now, then, let us be cool. Eula, you are not a green girl.

EULA. No; I'm a g-g-gushing old nuisance. (*Sobs.*)

JACK. Do not harp upon that. Let us forget all the wretched past, and live in the blooming present, and all that. You are the only girl—

EULA. You said that to them. (*Sobs.*)

JACK. Exactly. You are the only girl I ever loved, I said to each of those bold girls, and it was true, insomuch as I never could, would, or should love any girl at all.

EULA. I like that. (*Sobs.*)

JACK. I thought you would. Ah, Eula, you are the only mature woman I ever loved. You are the realization of my dreams, and all that. Be, oh! be my—

EULA (*starting up*). Oh, my lord! I will be your little wife.

Clasps him fondly around his neck, L., *while*
MRS. B. *embraces him*, R.)

JACK. Look here! I say! I meant be my mother. Oh, I say!

(*Enter* MARIA, CLORINDA, JENNIE, L.   *Stand amazed.*)

MARIA. He's done it this time, sure 'nuff.

QUICK CURTAIN.

ACT III.

(*Enter* MRS. B. ; *goes to mirror, arranges her bonnet ; sits on sofa ; plays solitaire.   Enter* MARIA, *counting money ; comes down front ; sits.*)

MARIA. Two dollars from Miss Capiani and two from Mrs. Norval is four, and one from Lord Jack is five, and Miss Eula's pink silk what she wore befo' the fall of Richmond. (*Ties money in handkerchief.*)   I 'ain't done badly, an' I ain't a-carin' now if no trains don't come at all.   I reckon pore Lord Jack feels different, though.   Mrs. Norval, she 'mos' died of laffing 'cause he got himself engaged to Miss Eula ; but Miss Capiani, she looked mightily sober-sided.   Yes, ma'am ; she's in love with him ; that's what !

(*Enter* CLORINDA, C.; *walks quickly to* MARIA.)

CLO. Maria, I want your help in a tremendous joke. You have a keen appreciation of satire, haven't you?

MARIA (*rising*). No, ma'am; I never use it.

CLO. Pshaw! I mean you like to see other people look silly.

MARIA (*laughing*). Oh, yes, indeed, ma'am.

CLO. Well, it's the same thing. First, this is for you. (*Gives her money.*)

MARIA. Lawsey me! you're sure 'nuff quality. Thank you, ma'am.

CLO. That's all right. Now I want you to manage to get Lord Jack behind this screen, and when he's there, come and tell me.

MARIA. But s'pose he won't go?

CLO. Won't go! Get him in here on some pretence, then tell him I'm coming, and suggest the screen as a hiding-place. You'll have no trouble.

MARIA. Lawsey me! What a merry lady you are, and how you do do that pore boy!

CLO. "That pore boy" needs a lesson. You'll find me in the office. (*Exit, laughing.*)

MARIA. Now what ever is she goin' to do?

8

(MRS. B. *comes behind her, taps her on shoulder, points after* CLORINDA.)

MARIA. Crickey! how you scared me! Go an' find out for yourself. (*Gesticulates violently. Exit* MRS. B.) There's a nice old bunch of curiosity—deaf an' dumb, an' f'rever pokin' an' pryin' like she was a magpie; an' I 'ain't never seen her face yet.

(*Enter* LORD JACK, C.)

MARIA. The very thing! Come here, your lordship.

JACK. Don't bother, Maria. You're pretty, and all that; but I've had a genteel sufficiency, as you say, of girls, pretty or otherwise. If a train don't come soon, I'll be a corpse. (*Sinks in chair by table,* L.)

MARIA (*patting him on the back*). Cheer up, my lord; if the worst comes to the worst, I can save you.

JACK. Nothing can save me but flight.

MARIA. Well, I know that. (*Whispers to him.*)

JACK. What if your brother has got a mule?

MARIA. You can run away on it for five dollars.

JACK (*jumping up*). Maria, you are an angel! When will it be ready?

MARIA. Whenever the money is.

JACK. Done! (*Gives her money.*) Now run. Have it at the side door, and when all is prepared, come— No, we must be cautious. Whistle this way (*whistles bugle call*), and I'll slip out.

MARIA (*makes several attempts to whistle; finally succeeds*). How's that? (*Goes to door*, c.)

JACK. Fine.

MARIA. Oh, hide! Quick! Get behind that screen. Mrs. Norval is comin' down the hall.

JACK. Gad, I'll run for it! (*Goes to door*, c.)

MARIA. Hush! She's here. (*Pushes him behind screen*, R. C.)

JACK. Remember the mule!

MARIA. Count on me. (*Winks to audience; comes down front.*) I'd as soon help him as any other; an' Mrs. Norval, she can try lookin' silly herself. Yes, ma'am; that what! (*Exit* c.)

(*Enter* CLORINDA, JENNIE, L.; *followed by* MRS. B., *who sits*, L., *facing screen*.)

CLO. (*going to* C.). I have a little business. proposition to make, Miss Capiani, and as it concerns Lord Jack, I presume you will be interested.

JEN. I knew you knew him.

CLO. Why shouldn't I ? I was once engaged to him. (*Laughs.*)

JEN. Jack engaged to a skirt dancer ! Impossible !

CLO. Ah ! but I'm not a skirt dancer. I'm just an ordinary goose of a girl like yourself, engaged in a most undignified pursuit.

JEN. I consider all this highly impertinent.

CLO. Keep cool. Come, let us sit down and talk reasonably. (*They sit*, C.) To be brief, here are you, I, and Miss Eula, all engaged to Lord Jack. Very good. You will admit we can't all marry him.

JEN. (*rising*). Oh, this is dreadful !

CLO. (*pulling her back*). Don't be a ninny, my dear. Any female under ninety can twist Jack around her finger, and if there were more girls here he'd be engaged to them all.

JEN. I suppose he would.

CLO. Undeniably. So why not enter into the affair in a business-like manner, as men do. We read of sugar trusts, wheat trusts, iron trusts; why not get up a Jack trust?

JEN. A Jack trust! What is a trust? I'm sure we've trusted Jack enough now. Too much.

CLO. Oh, in a trust, it's the other fellow who does the trusting, don't you see. Don't you ever read the newspapers?

JEN. No. Mamma says they are not fit reading for me.

CLO. Well, my mamma is broader in her views. Consequently I know several things which seem to have escaped your attention. Let me see how I can explain. First, some men get together all there is of some special article, and say, "Let's form a trust." That knocks the small dealer out of sight. Then the public trust the trust company, and the trust company trust each other until one of them skips to Canada, and that winds up the trust and the trust company. See?

JEN. No, I don't. What has this to do with Jack?

CLO. Good gracious! What a pity you never read the papers! Here! (*Rises; kneels on chair, facing* JENNIE.) There's only one Jack, who comes high, but all want him. Very good; you and I make a trust of him, and Miss Eula is out of the game. See?

JEN. Yes; that will be nice.

CLO. Then we run the trust till one of us gets him. See?

JEN. Oh! It's like a jack pot, isn't it?

CLO. Not a bit. There's no "anteing up." Besides, in poker, one jack don't make "a full house," while in this game he does. (*Laughs.*) That's pretty good for a girl. I wish there was some man here to take the point.

JEN. (*aside*). What a vulgar girl! (*Aloud.*) I hardly see your idea yet, Mrs. Norval.

CLO. Oh, sugar! I'll write out a neat little promise to marry for each of us. The first to find Jack alone presents it, wheedles him into singing it, and *voilà!* the Jack trust is dissolved. One skips with the boodle—Jack —and the other has the experience. See?

JEN. (*starting up*). Oh, you clever girl! And he couldn't run away after signing a paper?

CLO. Um! Well, I've heard of it being

done. But it would be a business-like affair, and relieve us of the necessity of being a fraction of a fiancée, which is degrading. (JACK's *head appears over top of screen.*)

JEN. It's just splendid! Write the agreement now.

CLO. (*going to table*, R., *sits;* JENNIE *behind her*). I'll take a page out of the register. (*Writes.*) " Whereas I, Jack Townley, being sane and of sound mind." How's that?

JEN. It sounds legal and binding.

CLO. Yes, it's legal, but it isn't true. Legal facts generally are not. (*Writes.*) "And most anxious to marry—" That's not even a legal fact, but it's necessary. (*Writes.*) "Do hereby desire and agree and consent to wed" —blank for name—"party of the second part, whenever she likes." Now how shall I end it?

JEN. Something about my seal, you know, and a red wafer.

CLO. Oh, yes! "Witness my hand and seal." Now for your copy. (*Writes rapidly.*) There! But we have no wafer.

JEN. (*taking out purse*). Would postage-stamps do?

CLO. They might make it seem more formal. Stick them on.

JEN. (*sticking on stamps*). Now I suppose the first one to catch Jack will be the lucky one? (*Looking around.*) I wonder where he is? (JACK'S *head disappears.*)

CLO. (*looking at screen*). I imagine he is not far away. (*Gives* JENNIE *paper.*) There is your copy. And now, *vogue la galère!* Each for herself, and the, etc., etc. (*Laughs.*) How nervous the dear boy would be if only he could hear our little plot!

JEN. Yes; wouldn't he? Shall we start now?

CLO. I'm ready. Which way are you going?

JEN. To the garden.

CLO. (*taking her arm*). So am I.

JEN. (*disengaging herself*). I meant up-stairs.

CLO. So did I.

JEN. Oh, dear! Excuse me, Mrs. Norval, but don't you see I want to go alone?

CLO. (*laughing*). So do I.

JEN. (*aside*). I can easily outrun her. (*Aloud.*) Pardon me for leaving you. (*Exit,* C., *running.*)

CLO. Poor girl! She's all broken up. I do hope she will find him. (*Very loud.*) I wonder where Jack can be? (*Looks at screen; goes to it; shakes it.*) He might be here. (*Winks at audience.*) No; he never could keep so still. I'll go hunt him up.

(*Exit, c., laughing and waving paper.* MRS. B. *follows.*)

JACK (*coming out, drops on sofa*). Jove! I feel like a confounded rabbit! Regularly hunted, and all that. It's all very amusing to be an irresistible, but I've gone a little too far. Of course that absurd paper amounts to nothing, as I could marry neither under existing circumstances, but I might sign it. In fact, I should sign it; I know I should. I simply cannot resist a woman. So my only hope is Maria and the mule.

(*Enter* CLORINDA, c., *waving paper.*)

JACK. Gad! (*Jumps up; runs across stage.*)
CLO. (*following*). Just a moment, Jack darling!
JACK (*running*). Can't stop. You're the only girl I ever loved.

(*Bolts out,* L., *pursued* by CLORINDA. *They
re-enter,* C., *cross stage* L. *to* R.; *back; exit,* L.
JACK *re-enters,* C., *out of breath; goes to* R.)

JACK. She's missed me; I doubled on her
in the hall.   Where *is* that mule?

(*Enter* JENNIE, L.; *runs to* JACK.   *They dodge
about stage while talking.*)

JACK. Very sorry, but I can't stop.
JEN. Oh, Jack, please wait.
JACK. You're the only girl I ever loved.
Let me be near thee.

(*Rushes out,* L., JENNIE *after, as* MARIA *enters,* C.)

MARIA (*holding up her hands*). My lawsey
me!   The mule's ready, and there he goes,
with that horrid gyurl chasin' him like he
was a 'coon!   I'll whistle to warn him.

(*Whistles bugle call.*   JACK, JENNIE, CLORIN-
DA *dash in; dodge around stage.*)

JACK (*breathlessly*). Can't stop.   (*Exit,* C.)
CLO. Hold on!   (*Exit,* C.)

(*Enter* EULA, L.; *stands amazed.*)

JEN. (*holding hand to her side*). Jack, wait! (*Exit*, C.)

MARIA. Crickey! what fun! (*Exit*, C., *whistling.*)

EULA. My poor dear boy! I'll tear their eyes out. (*Follows*, C.)

(*Enter* MRS. B., L.)

MRS. B. (*throws off sun-bonnet; slips out of old dress*). I'll take a hand myself, and save his fascinating life. (*Exit*, C.)

(JACK, CLORINDA, JENNIE, MARIA, EULA, MRS.
    B. *run in* L., *out* C., GIRLS *crying*, "Wait!"
    JACK, "Can't stop!")

MRS. B. (*re-entering*, L., *laughing*). It is too perfectly absurd!

(*Stands*, C. JACK, *entering*, L., *stops suddenly,
    facing her.* GIRLS, *following, stop in line
    slanting from* L. *to* C. *exit.*)

JACK. Clementine!

MRS. B. Yes, Jack, my dear. Pray present me to your friends, who have only known me as " old Mrs. Boothby."

JACK. You old Mrs. Boothby!

ALL. You?

MRS. B. (*laughing*). Yes, I. But pray present me, Jack.

JACK. Certainly, my darling. (*Crosses to her*, R. *Takes her hand.*) Ladies, let me present to you—my—er—er—ahem! wife.

ALL. Your wife?

JACK. Yes, my adorable wife. Oh, Clementine, you—you are the only girl I ever loved.

MRS. B. (*laughing archly*). So old Mrs. Boothby told me. Ah, Jack and ladies, I thank you very sincerely for the comedy you have played for me.

JACK. I knew you all the time.

MRS. B. Oh, you goose! But I forgive you.

JACK (*embracing her*). I knew you would. (*Bell rings.*) By Jove! the train.

JEN. What will mamma say?

CLO. Suppose we go and see.

EULA. I—I never could endure him. (*Faints.*)

MARIA (*placing her in chair*). Lawsey me! Hole up your head, Miss Eula. This ain't the first time you've been left, an' you orter be used to it. Yes, ma'am; that's what!

Mrs. B. Jack, shall we go?

JACK. Certainly, my darling. (*Advancing front.*)

> The joint-stock gone, the holders "bust,"
> The "Jack Trust" ends as all trusts must.
> .The moral is—you'll all agree—
> One *can* have too much luck like me.

TABLEAU.

MARIA.   CLORINDA. JENNIE.   JACK.

EULA.   MRS. B.

QUICK CURTAIN.

THE VENEERED SAVAGE.

CHARACTERS.

Lou Dayton .... *A Chicago belle.*

Madge Dayton .... *Her younger sister.*

Dick Majendie .... *Cousin to the sisters.*

The Duchess of Diddlesex.

Lady Fanny .... *Her daughter, a silent young person.*

Lord Algernon Penryhn ...... *Her son, a still more silent young person.*

Place, London.

THE VENEERED SAVAGE.

ACT. I.

Pleasant interior. Lou *and* Madge, *in ordinary house dress, reading a letter together as curtain rises.* *They read it, turn and look long at each other, as if in amazement, but still in silence.* Madge *walks towards back of stage,* Lou *still holding letter; throws letter angrily on table* l. f., *seats herself in chair* r. *of table.* *Knock at door.*

Madge (*turning*). Come!

(*Enter* Dick Majendie. *Both girls rush to him, each seizing an arm, they bring him down to foot-lights, exclaiming together* "Oh, Cousin Dick!"

Lou. Oh, Dick! I am so glad! You are the very man we want to see!

9

MADGE. Cousin Dick! My *dear* Dick! We did so want to see you!

DICK. Why that is just what Lou said. What is the matter that you both look so blue, and are so desperately fond of me? I never noticed anything of this kind in America. Are you home-sick already? or is something wrong about your luggage? Or perhaps you are not over the motion of the steamer yet. You came on the *Servia*, didn't you? I don't like the *Servia*.

LOU. Motion of the steamer—nonsense!

MADGE. Now, Dick, don't be stupid.

LOU. No, Dick; *don't* be dull.

DICK. But, girls—

MADGE. Can't you *see* we are angry?

LOU. Yes—furious!

(LOU *and* MADGE *talking together.*)

LOU. Yes, and I can just tell you—

MADGE. For my part, I will just say—

DICK (*who has been frantically turning from one to the other*). Oh, my poor ears! For Heaven's sake, girls, one at a time, *please!*

LOU. Well, I suppose you remember the son of the Duke of Diddlesex?

MADGE. You know, Dick, that red, gawky

young Englishman who visited us so long in
Chicago?

DICK. No. I know the Duchess very well,
but her son is on a hunting expedition—Norway, Africa, something of the sort—I have
never seen him.

LOU. My dear Dick, we are talking of
America. He visited us in Chicago. Why,
he was with us three months.

DICK. But I was here. You forget that I
have been in England the last two years.

MADGE. Never mind that; the point is we
have had a letter from the Duchess.

LOU. Yes, from the Duchess.

DICK. *The* duchess! Which? As an
American I am the fashion, and know as
many duchesses as Buffalo Bill.

LOU. Well, as *we* have only been in London one night, we only know one duchess—
by letter—the Duchess of Diddlesex.

MADGE. And to think that her son spent
two months with us—

LOU (*raising her voice*). *Three* months—

MADGE (*jerking* DICK *away by the arm,
and marching him up the stage and back*). It
is the most *outrageous* piece of business!

Lou (*jerking* Dick *by other arm, marching him away and back in same manner*). It is exactly what I have always heard of the English as a nation.   They are rude—

Madge. Pig-headed—

Lou. Sneering—

Madge. Supercilious !

Lou ⎫
Madge ⎭ (*both together*). ⎰ I despise them !
⎱ I hate them !

Dick. But why — what — where — how — what—what—*what* is it all about?   If you will kindly explain before I—

Lou (*seizing letter and crumpling it into his hand*). There ! read that !

(Dick *seats himself on table*, L. F.; Lou *sits* R. *of table;* Madge *stands* L. *of* Dick, *looking over his shoulder.*)

Dick (*reading*). " My dearest Sophie—" (*Stops short; stares.*)

Both Girls. Oh, go on ! go on !

Dick (*reading*). " Dearest Sophie, — You might not have known that you dine with me to-day *without fail* " (tremendously underscored), " but you do.   Consider me as a sinking ship, or what you please, in dire distress, and come to my rescue, whatever your other engagements. That is Kismet — at least it is mamma, which is the same thing, you know. I am now despatching a note of invitation to two Choctaw princesses from the West, Miss Louise Dayton and her younger sister, Madge—" (DICK *stops, whistles, stares at girls.*)

MADGE (*giving him a little shake*). Go on; the best is yet to come.

DICK (*reading*). "I forget precisely whether their native prairie village is called Detroit, Duluth, Kalamazoo, or Chicago. American geography is such a bore, with its barbarous nomenclature, one never can remember! One gets a little tired of Americans, except Buffalo Bill, who is charming. He never pretends to anything English. He reveals himself the simple aborigine. But the usual American girl—the veneered savage in the Worth gown, talking about her 'family' (save the mark!), coming here to waltz with the Prince of Wales, and hunt a possible husband among us — I am positively sick of her, and cannot see why our men rave so about American wit and beauty. For my part, I think they are simply pert and scrawny—"

Lou (*interrupting*). Sweet creature! How I burn to see her—and have her see me!

Dick. Hold on! here is the cream of the letter. Listen. (*Reads.*) "However, they are inevitable, these Choctaw ladies—at least Howard is peremptory about them. He has written again and again from Norway, not to mention a dozen telegrams, and is coming home simply to meet them. I have never known him so earnest about anything; as mamma says, he is evidently *épris* of one of them. Pleasant prospect for the House of Diddlesex, is it not? Still the prairie princess is not yet covered with our strawberry leaves, and before that is accomplished she will meet and reckon with mamma. Mamma says we are to humor Howard, *overwhelm* them with courtesies, play them as one does a trout, and at the right moment cut the whole affair short. But it is not necessary for me to notice them in any way. You understand, you are to come to talk to me, and we can amuse ourselves. Be sure you come to keep me in countenance and patience. Yours, as ever,

FANNY." A very pleasant note, upon my word! I never thought there was so much malice in Lady Fanny. She seems a jolly little soul; has been awfully kind to me, I assure you.

LOU (*sarcastically*). Of course, you are a *man*. I dare say she could even manage to recollect the name of your native prairie.

DICK. But how did this note come into your hands? Sophie is her sister-in-law, Lady Delancy, I fancy.

MADGE. That is simple. She wrote two notes at the same time. She says I *am* despatching a note of invitation. Don't you see — present tense? Very good; when all that spite and jealousy about American girls was poured out, there was nothing left in her but—her native idiocy; so she enclosed the notes in the wrong envelopes, and Sophie, whoever she is, is now reading our invitation to Diddlesex House, just as we have been reading hers.

LOU (*who has been walking about in a brownstudy*). I have it!

DICK. What?

LOU. An idea. She is tired of the regulation American girl—the veneered savage in a Worth gown, pretending to be English— and she likes Buffalo Bill. She shall have Buffalo Bill in petticoats—two of him—eh, Madge?

MADGE (*rushes down to* R.). Yes!

LOU. She shall have no cause to regret her Abyssinians.

MADGE (*clapping her hands*). We will go Zulu!

LOU. Have you told them anything about us yet, Dick?

DICK. Not a word. But if you seriously mean a masquerade—

LOU. Bright boy! That is precisely it.

DICK. It would be very undignified, and you never could carry it out.

MADGE. Oh, couldn't we? I have not forgotten my school-days yet. (*Gives an infantine yodle, skims across the stage and back.*) There, isn't that something in the style of a prairie princess?

LOU. But, Dick (*coaxingly*), *dear* Dick, there are some things you must tell us.

MADGE. Yes; slang, you know, and all that. I have one of Bret Harte's California stories and an article on " Bucolic Dialect of the Plains," which we can study up ; but the only bit of slang I remember just now is— playing it—er—playing it rather low down.

DICK. That is exactly what you two girls intend to do.

LOU (*pouting*). Never mind him, Madge ; we can read Bret Harte for ourselves between now and this evening, and learn enough in half an hour to astonish Lady Fanny. But there is something you must explain, Dick, and that is poker ; the terms, I mean—two of a kind, and all that. Papa would not allow us to learn the game.

DICK (*teasingly*). Then it is quite impossible. I could not explain my conduct to my uncle if I did.

MADGE. Nonsense ! You care so much, no matter what papa might say ! Come away, Lou. Don't you see we shall get no assistance from him ?

DICK. No ; I disapprove of the whole affair.

LOU. My dear cousin Dick, have we asked for your approbation ? This is our undertaking. But as a gentleman I presume you will keep silence.

DICK (*haughtily*). You presume!

MADGE (*soothingly*). Of course he will be silent, Lou.   He is an American, is he not? and are American men ever anything but gallant and courteous to women?   "Strawberry leaves," indeed!   (*Walking angrily up and down.*)   An honest, well-bred American gentleman (*seizes* DICK *by the arm*) is worth every ducal coronet in England.

(*Marches* DICK *across stage.*)

DICK (*laughing*). Thanks, my little cousin. What man would not prize a true-hearted American girl?

LOU (*following them impatiently*). Never mind heroics, but listen.   Fortune is propitious to us.   I have just remembered that we have with us the very gowns for the occasion. Our Mexican costumes, you know, Madge.

DICK. You will never wear those costumes here—to Diddlesex Castle?   Oh, girls, girls, do reflect!

LOU. My good cousin Dick, don't you see that is just what we are doing?   I am about it this moment; for, of course, we must have *sobriquets*.

DICK (*stupefied*). *Sobriquets?*

MADGE. Of course. Don't you see? *Sobriquets* to match the gowns. Something glaring and impossible. I have it!

LOU AND DICK. Well?

MADGE. Lightning Lou—(*all laugh*)—and Mashing Madge. Aren't they just too deliciously vulgar!

DICK (*laughs heartily, then suddenly grows serious*). This is all very droll here. But, girls—Lou, Madge—consider how strange! how unladylike!

LOU. Spare your remonstrances. It is done settled. I shall send those names up on our cards.

MADGE (*dancing about*). Yes, yes. Lightning Lou and Mashing Madge! Oh, what a joke!

LOU. You see, Dick, we are quite determined. There is only one course left for you —to be there in good season, and lose none of the fun.

MADGE. And pray, to avoid monotony, why should I not play the well-known American spoiled child, the overgrown girl who hardly knows her letters, has no manners, and should be in short skirts, but who is already in society and has love affairs. I'll *do* it!

(DICK *shrugs his shoulders, and walks to door.*)

Lou. But—an awful thought!—the duchess and her daughter have called, but we were not at home, and this note to Sophie—well, it speaks of dinner. Was it to dine we were asked?

DICK. Yes, to dine at eight. I am sure, for I was invited to meet you. (*Recollecting himself.*) Now, why did I tell you? If I had not, you could not have gone.

Lou. So sorry.

MADGE (*sweeping him a courtesy*). *Au revoir*, cousin. (*Goes to door with* Lou. *Exit* Lou, MADGE *coming back.*) You are not really angry, are you, cousin? I should hate to think you were really displeased.

DICK. My dear little Madge, it would be hard to be really angry with you. I am vexed, in an elder-brother way, with your folly, that is all. Even now, it is not too late.

MADGE (*running away to door*). Yes, it is,

Dick, much too late. Nothing would persuade me not to repay that contemptuous young woman in her own coin, and show her whether American hospitality is designing or not, and whether we entertained her brother out of hearty good-will or no. I fancy we shall succeed in making it clear to her how highly we two Choctaws value the strawberry leaves and other Diddlesex accessaries without good-will.

(*Waves her hand, gives* DICK *a mocking bow, goes out laughing.*)

DICK. Were there ever such madcaps! And they will do it; there's not a doubt of that. They'll carry it out. I won't go! I'll be ill—dead—out of town. Hang it! I will go, if only to see fair play. (*Lights a cigar.*) I must smoke on all this. In their Mexican dresses. (*Puffs at cigar, walks about.*) Lightning Lou and Mashing Madge. Atrocious! And the Duchess of Diddlesex, that most proper woman, she will never recover from the blow. And Lady Fanny! Who would suppose that little person could show so spiteful! (*Paces up and down again.*)

Gad, what a hateful letter! and how hard on the girls! Amazing how women claw each other. I am half inclined— By Jove, I will! Why not? (*Laughs.*) You will be Buffalo Bill in petticoats, will you, my pretty cousins? Then, pray, why not I Buffalo Bill himself — a ranch king, rather, or prairie prince, in huge hat, gay sash, pistols, etc.? Why not? The duchess shall infer that I am like the educated African, who goes back to his breech-cloth and savagery at the first tap of the Voudoo drum. I'll blossom out as the American aborigine at the first glimpse of my prairie cousins. Good! Excellent! It will be worth it all to see Lou and Madge on their first glance at me. (*Goes out whistling.*)

CURTAIN.

ACT II.

Handsome interior at Diddlesex Castle. Curtain rises on DUCHESS, LORD ALGERNON PENRYHN, *and* LADY FANNY, *in dinner dress, grouped at* R. C. *of stage opposite entrance on* L. FOOTMAN *announces* " MR. MAJENDIE." DICK *enters in wide sombrero, pistol and knife in red sash, high boots and spurs, wide collar, loose jacket. He affects a theatrical swagger, bows low to the group.*

DUCHESS (*eying him through her glass*). Mr. —er—Mr. Majendie!

LADY FANNY. Or one of Tussaud's waxworks.

LORD ALGERNON PENRYHN (*staring through monocle*). By Jove!

DICK (*bowing*). Dick Majendie, as much at your service as ever, Duchess. I have merely returned to my native costume. I saw my American cousins this morning—

LADY FANNY (*to nobody in particular*). Ah, that explains.

DICK (*turning quickly*). I beg your pardon.   You said—

LADY FANNY. Nothing, Mr. Majendie. You are quite mistaken.

DICK (*bows, and turns to* DUCHESS). Consider me, Duchess, as a victim to—

(*Enter* FOOTMAN *bringing cards.* DUCHESS *looks at them as if petrified, re-examines them, hands them to* DICK.)

DUCHESS. How very extraordinary!   Perhaps you can explain these — er — singular names, Mr. Majendie?

DICK (*reads aloud*). " Lightning Lou, *née* Dayton ; Mashing Madge, *née* Dayton."

LORD ALGERNON PENRYHN. By Jove!

LADY FANNY. Doubtless another American peculiarity.

DICK (*aside*). Spiteful little creature! (*Aloud.*) Precisely, as you say, another American custom.   Perhaps we should not presume to have ways of our own; but if you find us very barbarous, remember that we cannot all be born in England, you know.

LADY FANNY (*to her brother*). He never was so disagreeable before.   It is all the doing of those intolerable American cousins. I know it.

LORD ALGERNON PENRYHN. By Jove!

(FOOTMAN *announces loudly*, "LIGHTNING LOU, *née* DAYTON; MASHING MADGE, *née* DAYTON.*")

DICK (*coming down* L. F.). Ye gods!

(*Enter* LOU *and* MADGE *brilliantly dressed in Mexican costumes, skirts clearing ankles, showing Suède slippers, black lace stockings, short scarlet jackets embroidered with gold opening over white silk shirts, and black-and-gold sashes, dagger and pistol worn on chatelaine, large piece of lace or gauze worn on head as mantilla.* MADGE *wears flowing hair ; both have a profusion of Rhine-stone jewelry, and carry large fans, which they use with much coquetry.* MADGE, *without noticing anybody in room, saunters about examining bric-à-brac.*)

LOU (*advancing, assured and condescending*). The Duchess of Diddlesex, I presume. So glad to meet you, and your sister (*glances at* LADY FANNY)—no, daughter, is it not? Though we hardly thought we could spare

10

time to come to you. There is so much else that is *really* interesting. (*Fans herself and stares hard.*)

LORD ALGERNON PENRYHN. By Jove!

LADY FANNY. What savages!

DICK (*laughing aside*). One for the Duchess.

MADGE (*turns abruptly*). Walk light there, Lou. Of course the Duchess knows how it is herself. But (*to* DUCHESS), as I told Lou, we had heard so much of you from Howard.

DUCHESS. Howard!

MADGE. Yes, Howard! He is your son, isn't he? Howard Diddlesex. And he talked so much about you and the old gentleman—

DUCHESS. The old gentleman!

DICK (*coming forward*). My cousin means the Duke, I fancy.

(Lou *and* MADGE *look at* DICK *and start.*)

Lou (*aside to him*). You are a dear good fellow!

MADGE. Your cousin, Dick Majendie, means, as she generally does, just about what she says. And as I was saying, Duchess, I told Lou we'd just chip right in, in a sociable way. So you needn't trot out your company ways for us. (Lou *and* Dick *laugh aside.*)

Duchess. Company ways! Chip right in! I do not quite follow.

Lou. Oh, Duchess, you must pardon my little sister's school-girl slang; she is only fourteen, you know.

Lord Algernon Penryhn (*staring through glass*). By Jove!

Lady Fanny. Only fourteen; nonsense!

Madge (*giving a skip*). Good-sized girl, ain't I?

(Lady Fanny *turns disdainfully away.* Dick *draws* Madge's *arm protectingly through his.*)

Lou (*fanning herself and eying* Lord Algernon Penryhn *with marked coquetry*). Only fourteen, I assure you, Duchess, and, as you see, irrepressible. Indeed, that is why we came abroad, she had so *many* love affairs.

Duchess (*horror-struck*). So many love affairs! A girl of fourteen! Are such things possible in your country?

Lady Fanny (*aside*). The *East* Indian savages marry at *nine* years of age.

Madge. You bet they are, Duchess. (*Skips over to her side.*) Why, ma and pa were regularly rattled. They calculated I was sure to marry Jack Peyton. So I was, only (*pokes* Duchess *with her fan*) ma said I might come over here, and pa promised me a diamond necklace that should lay all over Flossie Skegg's—I mean her last one, that she does her marketing in.

Duchess. I do not comprehend. What is doing her marketing?

Lou. Why, ordering in the meat for dinner, and the garden sass, green things, milk, and eggs, you know. (*Aside to* Dick.) How was that, Dick? Madge outshines me in this line.

Lady Fanny. And you order groceries and—truck—in diamonds?

Madge (*impertinently*). We order groceries in paper bags; but we certainly wear our diamonds when we do it, if that is what you mean. No *lady* in Chicago would go shopping in *less* than $1500 worth of diamonds.

Lord Algernon Penryhn. Oh, by Jove!

Lou (*turning sharply on him*). An excellent country for penniless younger sons—to marry in.

Lady Fanny (*aside*). Insolent creature!

Lord Algernon Penryhn (*struggles with a speech, opens his mouth, shuts it, says again*). By Jove!

Duchess (*courteously to* Madge). I noticed you were looking at that little copy of Michael Angelo's—

Madge. Michael Angelo? Oh yes, I know. He painted that portrait of E. P. Strong; you know, Lou, Strong, the pork-packer.

Duchess. Oh! ah! doubtless another person—

(Lou *interrupts her by singing a refrain from* "*Erminie.*" Duchess *stops in marked manner; draws herself up.*)

Lou (*speaking over her shoulder*). Excuse me, Duchess; but, you see, we are untrammelled children of the West. *Prairie princesses*, as it were. (*Glances at* Lady Fanny, *who starts.*) I am afraid we shock you.

Duchess (*courteously*). Oh, not at all. But may I show you some of my paintings?

Here is a prairie scene that may interest you.

Lou (*skips up, hooks her arm within the* Duchess's). Prairie! I should smile! Just say prairie, and I'm all there. You understand, a prairie gets me.

(*They go out,* Duchess *doing the amiable.* Dick *and* Lord Algernon Penryhn *converse* l. c. Madge *takes* c. *of stage; stands contemplating* Lady Fanny, *who is seated* r. c.)

Madge. Are you ill?

Lady Fanny. Certainly not.

Madge. Have you any broken bones?

Lady Fanny (*haughtily*). I do not understand you.

Madge (*swaggering about*). I dare say. You English are a sort of kitchen nation. You know all about eating, running country-houses, keeping weekly accounts, making rich marriages, and stamping on poor people.

Dick (*crossing*). For Heaven's sake, Madge—

Madge. All right, Dick; it's not her fault, I know, if she was born an English girl. But do you always sit like this (*imitates* Lady

Fanny's *rigid pose*), and look like this?
(*Jumps up.*) Isn't there any *girl* in you?

Dick (*aside*). It's coming. There will be
a pitched battle, and I, as the neutral party,
shall be the victim, and taken away in sec-
tions.

Lady Fanny. Perhaps not, as you understand it.

Madge. But do you never snap your fingers, and jump and run (*suits action to word*),
and speak out and up, and go in for fun generally? (*Dances about.*)

Lady Fanny (*stiffly*). I *hope* not.

Madge. She *hopes* not. (*Laughs heartily.*)
She hopes she's a petrified fish. It's too
much for me. You talk to her, Dick, until
Lou comes back; she makes me tired.
(*Aside to audience*). I really did not know I
could be so rude and slangy.

(*Goes towards* Lord Algernon, *while* Dick
   crosses to Lady Fanny. Duchess *and* Lou
   enter.)

Lou (*talking eagerly*). Buffaloes! buffaloes!
Why, they are as thick in Chicago as—let
me see—as flies; aren't they, Dick?

DICK. What? Buffaloes in— Oh! ah! Yes, certainly. Quite so.

(MADGE *becomes convulsed with laughter behind her fan.*)

DUCHESS. I wonder you live where there are such dangers.

LOU. Dangers? Not at all. It's delightful. Chicago's no (*with an effort*)—no slouch of a city.

MADGE (*aside to* DICK). Poor Lou! she finds it hard — the elegant Miss Dayton, noted for her perfect manners. I must go to the rescue. (*To* DUCHESS.) Delightful! I should think so! There is no fun in the world up to a buffalo hunt. We were on one just before we came here, Lou and I.

LORD ALGERNON PENRYHN. By Jove!

DUCHESS. You confound me!

MADGE (*walking up and down, and slashing a little riding-whip she has taken from her belt*). Yes; just before we sailed. We were at breakfast, seven o'clock, I reckon—we have late breakfast at our house — when Will— er— (*She hesitates.*)

DICK (*aside to her*). Pajama will do. (*Laughs.*)

MADGE. —Will Pajama jumped in through the window, shouting, "Girls! girls! get your guns! A Buffalo hunt! Three hundred head of them at least, right outside the Palmer House!" "Oh, you hire a hall!" says Lou. (LOU *and* DICK *laugh together.*) And says he, "Honest Injun! See for yourself. The whole Stock Exchange is after them, half a dozen prayer-meetings, and every clerk in every shop that can beg, borrow, or steal a horse. Good time to say howdy to the folks."

LADY FANNY. Say what?

MADGE (*whirling on her*). Howdy, dear? We haven't time to drawl out, "How do you do?" (*To* DUCHESS.) As I was saying, Will said, "Get your lariats." As if we ever were without them! (*Rushing to* DICK.) Tell me, quick, where do those dreadful cowboys carry their lariats?

DICK. Around their necks, dear.

MADGE. We always wear our lariats around our necks at home. (DICK *in quiet convulsions of laughter.*) And it was just one jump from the breakfast-table—whiz! bang!—out of the house. Ma screaming, "Girls, come back! You'll get killed!" Lou tore the door open; I behind her, on the run. There was Lightning, Lou's horse, and Pitchfire, my pony. We always keep them ready saddled, you know, in case we should feel like taking the town—

Duchess. What *is* that?

Lou. Taking the town? Oh, when we feel bored, we ride up and down, half a dozen or so of us, giving the Comanche yell, and firing pistols now and then. You've no idea how it wakes one up.

Duchess. I should fancy it might.

Madge. Oh, but that isn't a patch on a buffalo hunt. Imagine it! Our horses are as fit as we, just mad to be off, whinnying and pawing. One jump to our saddles, and we're off. Lou's hair falls down. On we go, up one street, down another. Shrieks, cries, whoops, yells! Every one galloping like the wind, past Annie Dickson's, round the church corner; men cheering and shouting, and just ahead a great dark, heaving, bellowing mass—the buffaloes. Then Lightning and Pitchfire hump themselves, we whipping and screaming, just as mad as every one else.

(*Here* Lou *begins to gesticulate, and* Dick *gives a shout, as though carried away by excitement; both follow* Madge's *description with appropriate gestures.*)

Madge. Out goes the lariat—

Dick. Hi! hi! Steady!

Madge. Straight as a shot, pliable as a rope; turning, twisting, drawing, pulling, and he is down on his knees helpless, the biggest buffalo of the herd. That was my cast, and that is what *I* call living.

Dick (*aside*). Bravo, Madge! You're a positive genius.

Lady Fanny (*aside*). For a Comanche— yes.

Lou. Don't be startled, Duchess, my little sister is so impulsive; but then we are all so excitable on the subject of—er—buffaloes; they take the place of foxes with us, with the added zest of danger. Of course, very few girls make such a ten-strike as Madge; and you bet pa is proud of it. He had that buffalo's horns cased in gold, tipped with sapphires, engraved with Madge's name, the date, etc., and hung up in the hall.

DUCHESS. And you mean to say that these monsters are often seen in the very streets of Chicago? Where do they come from?

DICK. They come from St. Louis generally, a sort of suburb to Chicago. (*Laughs to Lou.*) That is the reason the girls go heeled.

DUCHESS. Heeled! What is that?

MADGE (*tapping her weapons*). Armed, he means. Any time you are out shopping, you may see a hundred head of buffaloes tearing down the avenue, trampling everything flat before them. No stops for refreshments; so it is well to be ready.

DUCHESS. Horrible! And to think that Howard remained there three months!

LOU. That is the reason all the nurses in Chicago are men; no female could get a child out of the way in time. It is all a smart man can do to get the children safely to and from the City Playground, where they are obliged to play by law.

DUCHESS. Play by law?

MADGE. Why, of course; even our aldermen could not allow the little innocents to play about streets, door-steps, or gardens, liable to be stamped by buffaloes at any moment.

(DICK *goes off in a wild fit of laughter.*)

DUCHESS (*severely*). I see no reason for mirth. (*Shudders.*) It must be a dreadful country.

LADY FANNY. It is strange Howard said nothing of this.

LOU (*innocently*). Did he not? That is odd indeed.

MADGE. Oh, come off, Lou! I'm dead tired of all this talking, and besides—

LOU. Yes, of course; we are expected to show up at Lady Monteith's.

DUCHESS. Lady Monteith's, young ladies, when you dine with me, and dinner is about to be announced?

MADGE (*dropping her burlesque manner*). I am sure you will pardon us, Duchess, but we are savages, you know, and only eat bread and salt with our well-wishers, not to mention that we shall hardly find time to get into proper dinner gowns and drive to Lady Monteith's.

DUCHESS. I do not comprehend you, Miss Dayton.

MADGE. It is very simple, Duchess. You, or perhaps I should say your daughter, Lady Fanny, preferred something in the Zulu or Choctaw style—prairie princesses, pure and simple, the genuine American *à la* Buffalo Bill—and we have been doing our best to enact the part.

LOU. While Lady Monteith only expects the *veneered savage* in the Worth gown.

LORD ALGERNON PENRYHN. By Jove!

DUCHESS (*looking at* LADY FANNY). What is all this? I am bewildered!

LOU (*holding out* LADY FANNY's *note*). If any further explanation is needed, this note may supply it. (*To* DUCHESS.) It was written apparently by Lady Fanny, and by an unfortunate accident enclosed, instead of an invitation to dinner, in an envelope directed to me.

LADY FANNY (*snatches note*). Good gracious! My note to Sophie!

DUCHESS. What will Howard say?

(*Both girls smile; courtesy low to* DUCHESS.)

DICK (*coming forward.*) Permit me also to say farewell, Duchess.

LADY FANNY. But, Mr. Majendie, you dine with us.

DICK (*bowing*). Pardon.   My cousins.

(DICK, MADGE, *and* LOU *retire backward to door.*)

LORD ALGERNON PENRYHN. By Jove!

(*Curtain falls on tableau.* DUCHESS *pointing to letter,* LADY FANNY *pouting,* LORD ALGERNON PENRYHN *staring through glass at the Americans, who are grouped in door, making their final bows.*)

TULU.

CHARACTERS.

THE DUCHESS OF TOEDMAG......*A law unto herself—and others.*

LORD BLAZONBERRIE.......*Her son, well descended of course, and still descending.   In love with " Old Bob's " Petroleum.*

JACK RYDER.....*An ascending American, in love with "Old Bob's" Petrolia, his cousin.*

PETROLIA SEERSUCKER......*" Old Bob's " eldest.   A charming American atrocity—" on approval."*

TULU SEERSUCKER.....*" Old Bob's " youngest.   An irrepressible American atrocity.   "Minds no one but papa."*

DICK CHETWYN.......*Nephew to the Duchess, a photograph fiend.*

ROBINSON.....*The butler, one of the props of the British Constitution.*

THE CAMERA.............*A most taking character.*

TULU.

ACT I.

Library in Toedmag Castle. Entrances with portières, c. and l.; fireplace across r. u. corner, sofa by it; desk with picture over it, r. f., two chairs near; tête-à-tête, c.; tea-table and seats l. u. corner, piano-lamp by it. Curtain rises on ROBINSON, *arranging tea-table.*

ROB. 'Ere's a state hof things! Lord Blazonberrie a-goin' to marry a Hamerican, hand the Duchess a-'oldin' 'is 'at. Hawful! puffectly hawful! The haristocracy hof Hengland is played hout, hand money rules the waves.

TULU (*running in*, c.). Holloa, Robinson, where's everybody?

ROB. The Duchess his hup in 'er hapartment; Lord Blazonberrie, Miss Seersucker, hand Mr. Ryder, his hout hin the kennels—

TULU. I know all that; I mean where's Mr. Dick?

ROB. Beg parding, miss, but you says, " Where's heverybody?" Hand Mr. Dick, 'e's not heverybody.

TULU. He's the only jolly one in the house. I never saw such a poky lot. I'm awfully hungry, give me some grub.

ROB. (*stiffly*). 'Elp yourself, miss. (*Passes wafers.*)

TULU (*taking handful*). Thanks. (*Curls up on sofa,* R.) I say, Robinson, you're what they call a feudal retainer, aren't you?

ROB. A w'ich, miss?

TULU. Feudal retainer. I mean you've been in the family years and years.

ROB. I've served the Toedmag family forty-one year, miss. I took service under the father of the present duke, Lord Blazonberrie's father.

TULU. Gracious! And was the Duchess here all the time? I wonder you are alive.

ROB. The Duchess 'as honly been hin hour family thirty-two year. She was the Lady

'Ildegarde Lyona Decima Hadela 'Unting-tower, the toast hand belle hof the west hof Hengland.

TULU. Toast *hand* belle, was she? Well, she's got nicely over that part. Thirty-two, and—she was pretty old when she married, wasn't she?

ROB. Couldn't hundertake to say, miss. (*Smiles.*)

TULU. You know she was. I bet she came over with William the Conqueror!

DICK (*outside*). Robinson!

TULU. Mr. Dick is coming! (*Jumps up.*)

DICK (*outside*). Lend a hand with this beastly camera.

ROB. Yes, sir; d'rectly, sir. (*Aside.*) Blow 'is beastly camery! (*Exit*, C.)

TULU. Now for some fun! (*Exit*, C.)

(DICK *enters*, C., *followed by* TULU, *carrying box;* ROBINSON *carrying camera.*)

DICK (*going to* L. F.). Set it down gently, facing the fireplace. (ROB. *places it backward,* L.) No, no, stupid—the other way! Don't get red in the face, Robinson, it don't suit your style of beauty. Where's that box of plates?

TULU. Here they are, Mr. Dick.

DICK. Tulu, I distinctly told you not to touch any of my things. Little girls should obey their elders. (*Business of arranging camera*).

TULU. Little girls! I'm fifteen, and I guess I could take pictures as well as you, even if you are eighteen. Saunders says you've spoiled sixty-eight plates this month.

DICK. Saunders is an ass. It was only sixty, and the fault of the plates every time.

TULU. Oh, Mr. Dick, *please* let me take a picture. I looked through the spy-hole this morning, and I know I could do it.

DICK. Oh, you did, did you? I'll trouble you not to look again; this camera cost money.

TULU. Thought it was given away with a pound of tea. (*Sits on tête-à-tête, c.*) Say, Mr. Dick, will you ever be a lord?

DICK. I hardly think so. My father blooms like a Christmas rose, not to mention three elder brothers.

TULU. That's too bad. You'd make a lovely lord.

DICK. Shouldn't I? Now, Tulu, I'll tell

you what you can do. Throw yourself into an attitude, and I'll take your picture, with Robinson in the background.

Rob. Beg parding, Mr. Dick, but I ain't particular about being took.

Tulu. Don't be a chump, Robinson. Everybody wants to be took.

Dick. Of course they do ; and a most lovable vanity it is to the amateur photographer. I say, Robinson, do you recollect the time Blazonberrie and I sent your picture to the cook, with a love-letter, and the jolly row we had ?

Tulu. Did she accept him, Mr. Dick ?

Dick. Like a shot. There's where the trouble came in. Those were great days, eh, Robinson ?

Rob. You was a most hawful larky boy, Mr. Dick.

Dick. Was I not ? And to think I should be the main-stay of your old age, and take your picture myself ! Queer !

Rob. Beg parding, but it certainly do seem queer for a young gentleman to mess with a picture-machine, like 'e was a cad hin a cart, taking 'em hoff hat shilling a 'ead.

Tulu. What stuff! Every one home has a Kodak.

Rob. His them the Hindians, miss?

Tulu (*laughing*). Them's the *Hindians*. (*Winks to* Dick.) They're like your "tigers" on this side. Here! I'll rig you up like our man Friday, and Mr. Dick shall take us.

Dick. I'm in that.

Tulu (*drapes* Robinson *in afghan, pins it, rolls his head in a tidy*). There you are! Now wave the tongs about.

Rob. S'pose her ladyship were to come in.

Tulu. She's wigging her maid up-stairs.

Dick. You're safe enough. Go over to the fire.

Tulu (*scowling furiously*). Now I'm the Duchess.

Rob. Lor, what a larky young lady! Ha! ha! ha! S'posing I were to prance habout a bit—so. 'Ow would that be? (*Prances.*)

Dick. Superb! You ought to go on the stage, Robinson. Keep your nose well curled, Tulu, and we'll call this "English lady watching a Kodak dance." (*Focuses.*)

Tulu. Keep on prancing, Robinson, and

I'll be saying, " Atrocious !" as the Duchess does. Now, then. Atrocious !

DICK. Capital ! One—two—

(*Enter* DUCHESS, L., *behind* DICK.)

DUCHESS. Atrocious !

ROB. (*dropping tongs*). 'Orror ! the Duchess !

TULU. What fun ! (*Kneels on tête-à-tête, facing* DUCHESS.)

DICK (*taking out his head*). What the deuce— Oh, Aunt Hildegarde, you've spoiled a plate.

DUCHESS (*eying* ROB. *through glass*). Robinson, remove that afghan.

ROB. (*tugging at afghan*). I 'umbly 'ope your ladyship will kindly overlook this. (*Aside.*) Blast the pins ! (*Aloud.*) Mr. Dick he inviggled me hinto hit. (*Aside.*) Hit won't come hoff !

DUCHESS. Am I to speak twice ? Remove those idiotic things.

ROB. They won't come hoff. (*Tugs.*)

DUCHESS. Then retire.

ROB. Yes, my lady. (*Exit*, C., *afghan dragging from coat-tails.*)

TULU. Oh, how funny! I shall die! (*Laughs.*)

DUCHESS. You are an ill-bred child, and should be in the school-room.

TULU. Child! I'm fifteen.

DUCHESS (*severely*). You will oblige me by finding your sister and telling her I am waiting, *waiting* tea for her.

TULU. I'll fetch her. (*Runs out, c., laughing.*)

DUCHESS (*sitting by table*). These girls are absolutely unendurable. That overgrown hoyden is bad enough, but her sister is—atrocious!

DICK (*sitting on tête-à-tête*). Miss Seersucker is immense.

DUCHESS. Immense! on the contrary, she is under-sized; all Americans are.

DICK. I meant she was no end jolly.

DUCHESS. Then why don't you speak English, and say so?

DICK. Because Amerikish is more expressive.

DUCHESS. Since your visit to the States you are low, Dick—positively flippant.

DICK. I say, Aunt Hildegarde, why don't

you let up on Miss Seersucker a bit? I don't see why you're always jumping on her.

Duchess. Because she is a most presuming young person, and her impertinence drives me wild. Yesterday she compared our "smart set" to her friends at home. Fancy!

Dick. They're much the same, except that while the natural British expression is smartly vacuous, the American has to repress an ill-bred intelligence and keenness from his features before he is good form.

Duchess. You are trying to be witty.

Dick. I always am witty. By-the-way, has Blazonberrie made any running with Miss Seersucker?

Duchess. He has not yet proposed, if you mean that. Of course, he must do it eventually, as his debts must be paid. But it's a sacrifice.

Dick (*rising; goes to fire*). Sacrifice!

Duchess. What else would you call it? This girl's father is called "old Bob" in those American newspapers. I have seen an article myself, giving a sketch of his life, with a woodcut of a wide-mouthed man, headed, "Old Bob Interviewed." Of course he eats pie for breakfast, with his knife; all Americans do. And he says (*lowers voice*) "By the jumping Moses!"—Blazonberrie heard him.

DICK. What a catalogue of crimes!

DUCHESS. Is it not fearful? Think of poor Blazonberrie with such a father-in-law! Picture that atrocious creature sitting here chewing tobacco and telling how he entered New York a barefoot boy, and now rolls out in his private car!

DICK. Yes, with the Duke opposite telling how he fattened up his prize hogs.

DUCHESS. The Duke's disgusting fad does not excuse the coarseness of this American. Poor Blazonberrie!

DICK. Jove! Blazonberrie is by way of having luck. If old Bob pays sixty thousand pounds for him, and gives him his pretty daughter, he isn't a bad old chap. Hand-made and a bit rough, but better for wear than some of our "hand-me-down" dukes.

DUCHESS. Hand-me-down dukes!

DICK. Yes; a lot of fellows all cut after the same devilish old and bad pattern, waiting to be sold.

DUCHESS. You had better call yourself an anarchist at once, Dick.

DICK. I'm too fond of soap and water to be an anarchist, not to mention—

(*Enter* BLAZONBERRIE, C.)

BLAZ. Take yourself off a moment, will you, Dick? I want a word with the Duchess.

DICK. Certainly. I'll join the others. (*Aside.*) A row. (*Exit*, c.)

DUCHESS. What is the trouble now, Blazonberrie?

BLAZ. (*going to fire*). Simply that you must manage to control your beastly temper, and be more civil to Miss Seersucker.

DUCHESS. My beastly temper! (*Rises.*)

BLAZ. Yes. You invite the girl here to give me a chance to propose, then insult her steadily. Regarded as a mother-in-law, you are absolutely appalling.

DUCHESS (*sits on tête-à-tête*). Oh, blame me.

BLAZ. I certainly will. Then there's Ryder. Could you not see he was dead spoons on Miss Seersucker? What did you ask him for?

DUCHESS. Because I did not wish any cligible men here to interfere with you. He is quite a lion since his book came out; and, being the Seersucker person's cousin, is out of the field.

BLAZ. Third cousins can marry.

DUCHESS (*fanning herself*). Nonsense! This girl has been sent here to marry a title; yours is the best in the market; it is quite a matter of business. She could as well stay at home if she were to marry her cousin.

BLAZ. Well, go on, go on, and when you've driven her from the house, do not be amazed if I do something desperate.

DUCHESS (*starting up*). Great heavens! you do not mean to marry an actress!

BLAZ. No; I mean to earn money for myself.

DUCHESS. You do not know how.

BLAZ. I can drive. I will put the racing stud into harness, start a livery-stable, and drive a hansom myself. It's quite the thing now to support yourself.

DUCHESS. Think of the disgrace to the family!

BLAZ. Think of the fun for me!

DUCHESS. This girl shall marry you. I will crawl, cringe, flatter—anything to prevent such a disgrace. A Toedmag earn money! Atrocious! (*Laughter outside.*)

BLAZ. They are coming in. Now recollect yourself. Talk! Yes, I fancy to - morrow would be a good day—

(DUCHESS *goes to tea-table. Enter* PETROLIA, DICK, RYDER, *and* TULU, C.)

BLAZ. We were speaking of our trip to the Abbey, Miss Seersucker. How would to-morrow do? Allow me. (*Helps her take off her wraps.*)

PET. Thanks. Any day will be delightful. I adore ruins. That's why I'm so fond of the English aristocracy.

BLAZ. (*laughing*). We are thankful to be liked for any reason. At least, I am. (*Goes to fire.*)

(TULU, JACK, *and* DICK *follow; talk.*)

PET. Duchess, Tulu tells me I have kept you waiting. Pardon me, and blame those fascinating puppies. Don't you just perfectly adore puppies? (*Sits on tête-à-tête.*)

DUCHESS (*severely*). Young ladies did not affect mannish tastes in my day, Miss Seersucker.

PET. I see : not being born in the dog-days, you let the men go to the dogs alone. Our ancestresses were a slow crowd, don't you think ?

DUCHESS (*eying her through glass*). *Our* ancestresses ?

PET. Pardon ; I meant *mine.* I forget who you were before the Duke married you. Were you anybody ?

DUCHESS. I, anybody !

PET. Yes. It's so puzzling over here to meet three or four hundred pounds of woman, with a society smile and a Felix gown, and be told it's "nobody." Makes one feel like a trance medium, don't you think ?

(ROB. *brings in kettle, muffins, lights spirit-lamp, retires.*)

DUCHESS. I know nothing of such people.

PET. What's the matter with Madam Blavatsky ?

DUCHESS. I have not heard that anything ailed her, and fail to see your point.

PET. Points are made with a brad-awl over here, I notice.

DUCHESS. Atrocious!

PET. Oh, you were born so. There's my receipt for punch.

BLAZ. (*coming forward*). What sort, Miss Seersucker?

PET. *London Punch*, my lord. No one ever gets the idea.

BLAZ. I am sure we could not fail to, mother.

DUCHESS. Certainly. Pray tell us it.

PET. To one evaporated British joke add four quarts of the milk of human-kindness. Keep in a dark, dry place for a year till it swells to ten pages. Garnish with Pears' Soap ads., and there you are.

DUCHESS. Atro—um—very bright. (*Pours tea.*)

BLAZ. Deuced clever. Capital! (*Laughs.*)

PET. (*crossing to fire*). What's going on over here?

BLAZ. What the deuce did she mean? (*To* DUCHESS.) Call Ryder away from her.

DUCHESS. Mr. Ryder, may I give you a

12

cup of tea? Blazonberrie, hand this to Miss Seersucker. Dick, help Miss Tulu.

(BLAZONBERRIE *carries tea to* PETROLIA. RY-
DER *comes to table.*)

JACK. No cream, Duchess. Thanks. (*Starts to fireplace again.*)

DUCHESS. Sit down here, Mr. Ryder.

JACK. Delighted, Duchess. (*Sits staring at* PET.)

(DICK *and* TULU *come to table.*)

DICK. Are you in this, Tulu?

TULU. Yep. Have some tea " on me."

DICK. A cupful of sugar, and a lump of tea, Aunt Hildegarde.

TULU. Oh, come off, Mr. Dick, I'm not a baby. No sugar at all, Duchess; just a slice of lemon, as Smithy takes it.

DUCHESS. Why do you call your sister Smithy?

TULU. Oh, just for roots, Duchess.

DUCHESS. What language does this child speak?

DICK. Amerikish, Aunt Hildegarde. Come over here, Tulu.

(*He and* TULU *sit by desk. Business of quarrelling over tea and muffins.*)

JACK. Tulu amazes you, Duchess, does she not? She is a nice little thing, barring her slanginess.

DUCHESS. I simply do not comprehend her. But I wish to tell you, Mr. Ryder, how very pleased I am to have you here. To me authors, artists, musicians, and even actors are very interesting.

JACK. You are very kind, Duchess.

DUCHESS. No, I am simply broad in my views—much more so than the Duke—and I study human nature in *all* classes.

JACK. Pardon, my cousin has no muffins. (*Rises, takes plates.*)

DUCHESS. Blazonberrie will wait upon her. But come into the drawing-room; I have a great deal to say to you. Come.

JACK. Delighted.

(*Exit,* L., *with* DUCHESS.)

PET. Where are they going?

TULU. The Duchess is going to pump Jack.

PET. Tulu!

TULU. You can't down me, Smithy. You're only four years older than I.

BLAZ. Declaration of Independence number two.

TULU. Yes; I only mind papa. Say, Smithy, tell our fortunes.

PET. Anything to keep you quiet. Please get me a pack of cards, Lord Blazonberrie. (*Comes forward to tête-à-tête.*) Who will be first?

DICK. My face is my fortune.

TULU. Rough luck, isn't it, Mr. Dick?

DICK. I say, I thought we were chums.

PET. Tulu, you are rude.

DICK. Never mind. (BLAZ. *stands behind* PET.; *winks to* DICK.) What are you winking for, Blazonberrie?

BLAZ. Something in my eye. (*Gives cards to* PET.)

DICK. In your eye!

TULU. What a noodle! Come on up-stairs. (*Pulls him down* F.) Four is a regular *jam.* He wants to see Petrolia alone. Get the idea? *Alone.*

DICK. By Jove! Tulu, wouldn't you like to help me fetch down the things? You know I am to take a flash-light picture. (*Aside.*) How was that—natural?

TULU. Elegant. Come on, and I'll squeeze the bulb. (*Runs out*, C. E.)

DICK. Not much! (*Follows*, C. E.)

BLAZ. May I hear my fortune now, Miss Seersucker? (*Sits on tête-à-tête.*)

PET. Certainly. Shuffle the cards, cut three times with your left hand, and keep your mind on your wish, your best. (*Gives him cards.*)

BLAZ. (*shuffling cards*). I have but one wish, as you know, Miss Seersucker.

PET. I? Oh, dear, no. You forget I've only known you three months.

BLAZ. (*sentimentally*). It seems like years.

PET. (*coquettishly*). Thanks. I really had no idea I made time hang so heavily. How unkind to tell me.

BLAZ. You know what I mean.

PET. (*archly*). I wish I did.

BLAZ. What do you wish me to understand?

PET. All you conveniently can. But we must not keep Fate waiting. (*Takes cards, looks them over.*)

BLAZ. (*pulling his mustache*). Jove!

PET. How funny! Here is a horse.

BLAZ. In the cards?

PET. (*showing card*). There he is—a trotter. He is to race; there is money on him; but beware! following him come disappointment and loss of money.

BLAZ. You are a witch, Miss Seersucker. Is he a bay, or can't you tell?

PET. The cards tell everything. He is a blonde. Beware of a red roan steed. See, here is the red roan steed card. (*Shows card.*)

BLAZ. It must be Cutaway.

PET. Doubtless it is. Don't back him.

BLAZ. I have, worse luck!

PET. Never mind; here is a blond woman with a good heart for you. You seem to run to blondes. She brings you money. Oh! such lots and lots of money! Who is she? Have you a blond aunt, and has she money?

BLAZ. I'd rather have her heart.

PET. Your aunt's?

BLAZ. No, no; you—the girl's in the cards. Do I get my wish?

PET. I think not. A tall, dark woman interferes, and the end is — disappointment. (*Rises.*)

BLAZ. (*rising*). Miss Seersucker—Petrolia! Tell me, is there anything between you and Ryder?

PET. (*looking down*). Between Jack and I? Er—well, yes, there is—

BLAZ. Engagement? Understanding?

PET. Oh no. Only a portière, and the Duchess's head. That is all. Why do you ask?

BLAZ. Then I may—er—don't you—

(TULU *and* DICK *enter*, C. E.)

TULU. Here we are again.

BLAZ. Oh, confound it! (*Goes to fire.*)

DICK. Call the others; we're all ready, Tulu.

TULU (*going to door*). Come on, Jack! Duchess!

PET. Everything all right this time, Mr. Chetwyn?

DICK. Yes, I have remembered everything. (*Business of arranging camera.*)

PET. Are you going to hold the plate in your hand? Is that a new way?

DICK. Oh, I am a thick head! (*Puts in plate.*)

(Duchess *and* Jack *enter.*)

Jack (*going to tête-à-tête*). Petrolia and I
will look well here, don't you think! (*Sits.*)

Pet. Yes; we'll sit here.

Duchess. Oh no! Miss Seersucker, be
kind enough to stand by Blazonberrie. Mr.
Ryder, you and I will stand here. (*Crosses
to* C. E.)

Jack. Delighted. (*Follows her.*)

Tulu. I'll sit here. (*Sits by desk.*)

Dick (*focusing*). This is immense. A go
from Goville!

Duchess. Dick, do not use those odious
Americanisms.

Jack. Pray consider our feelings as odious
Americans, Duchess.

Duchess. I do not refer to you, Mr. Ryder.
But I understand there are social stratas even
in the States, and Dick gravitates naturally
to the lowest.

Dick (*taking out head*). I like that!

Tulu. Mr. Dick got in with a lot of jays
at home, Duchess.

Duchess. And what is a jay?

Pet. Tulu, I insist on your being quiet.

TULU. Smithy, I won't. You know what a flubdub is, Duchess?

DUCHESS. Indeed, I do not.

JACK. My dear Tulu!

TULU. I'm awake, Jack. A flubdub is a no count fellow who don't pay his poker debts; and a jay is the same, only more so. Petrolia says there are lots of them over here, only you call them—

PET (*interrupting*). Jack, do stop her.

JACK. Tulu, you are rather young to lead the talk. (*Crosses, sits by her.*) Don't you see Chetwyn is waiting?

DICK. I should say I was. Now, Blazonberrie, close the blinds, and we're off. And for gracious' sake, don't wink when the flash comes.

(DICK *focuses, everybody poses,* BLAZONBERRIE *goes to window, is about to close blind, when* ROBINSON *enters, gives jewel-box and letter to* DUCHESS.)

ROB. Beg parding, your ladyship, but the young man from the bank brought these, and wishes a receipt.

DUCHESS. Place the box on the table. Blazonberrie, kindly write a receipt.

BLAZ. Certainly. (*Crosses to desk, writes.*)

DUCHESS. Dick, this absurd picture must wait.

DICK. Of course! I never saw such a jolly disobliging lot. (*Crosses to* TULU.)

(JACK *goes to fire, talks to* PETROLIA; *they turn their backs on room.* BLAZONBERRIE *gives receipt to* ROBINSON, *who retires.* DUCHESS *points to couple.*)

BLAZ. Jove! Call her over here.

DUCHESS (*opening box*). Miss Seersucker, would you care to see our family jewels?

PET. Indeed I should. I adore jewels. (*Comes to table, followed by* JACK.)

DUCHESS. Some of these have quite a history.

PET. That will interest you, Jack.

JACK. Yes, ancient jewelry is quite a fad of mine.

DUCHESS. This is modern; a gift from the Duke on my wedding-day. (*Hands her necklace.*)

PET. Oh, how perfectly gorgeous!

BLAZ. Come over to the glass and try them on, Miss Seersucker.

(*They go to mirror over fireplace;* BLAZONBER-
RIE *assists* PET. *to fasten necklace; she coquets
with him.*)

JACK (*aside*). That settles it. Diamonds
are trumps. Bah!

DUCHESS. Are you fond of diamonds, Mr.
Ryder?

JACK (*staring at* PET.). Never eat them—
oh, beg pardon, Duchess. But, really, I care
less for large stones than for quaint old set-
tings. Some of the old Russian or East Indian work is perfect.

DUCHESS. Then I have the very thing.
Lift out this tray, if you please. (*They bend
over box.*)

TULU (*jumping up*). Come on, Mr. Dick;
they don't want us. Hateful things!

DICK. They do not seem to miss us.

TULU. Come on, and we'll get *it*.

DICK. I'm with you. Hush!

TULU. Hush! (*They tiptoe off*, L. E.)

DUCHESS (*taking out case*). Are you a col-
lector, Mr. Ryder?

JACK (*laughing, detaches amulet from his
watch-chain*). There is my East Indian collection, Duchess. Compact, is it not?

DUCHESS. Very dainty. An amulet-box, is it not?

JACK. Yes, Duchess. (*Hands it to her.*)

PET. (*coming forward*). The necklace is adorable, Duchess. Ah, you have Jack's East Indian collection. Wouldn't it make a jolly stamp-box?

BLAZ. Or match-box?

JACK. Hear the vandals! Use a sacred amulet-box for matches!

PET. (*crossing to* JACK). I would like it, Jack.

JACK. Everything I have is yours. That "goes without saying."

PET. It does. It has gone a long time without saying.

JACK. I am in earnest.

DUCHESS. Now, young people, here is the gem of all my treasures—the Ranee's necklace; an heirloom with a most tragic history. (*Holds up necklace.*)

JACK. That is a treasure! Who could hesitate between that and a string of huge stones such as any parvenu can buy?

PET. It's perfectly adorable! See how the fire opal in the pendant gleams, Jack!

It seems almost alive. Do tell us the history, Duchess.

DUCHESS. Blazonberrie shall tell it. Mr. Ryder, sit by me. (*Gives* BLAZ. *necklace.*)

BLAZ. Be seated, Miss Seersucker. It is quite a long yarn.

PET. Delicious! Firelight, twilight, and a ghost-story. (*Sits on tête-à-tête.*)

(DUCHESS *and* RYDER *by table.* BLAZONBER-
RIE *stands,* C.)

BLAZ. (*holding up necklace*). This is the Ranee's necklace. Please to observe the four diamonds set about the pendant, for thereby hangs a tale of blood and woe. Somewhere in the days of Clive, Sir Guy Rommery, an ancestor of ours, went out to India to seek his fortune, and a jolly pile of loot—boodle—he scooped in.

DUCHESS. Blazonberrie, do not be so flippant.

BLAZ. Oh, you want something more dramatic? Werry good. Turn on the red light, thump the muffled drum, pick the string of the violoncello, for the tragedy is at hand. Scene: closing agonies at the taking of an

Indian city by the English. Tum-tum-tum, r-r-r-um, crash!

DUCHESS. How clever he is!

PET. Bring on the villain, Lord Blazon-berrie.

BLAZ. Here he is, sword in hand, surrounded by blood, flames, fire, and fury. Sir Guy breaks into the Ranee's apartment, where she stands undismayed among her cowering attendants, and, alas! her white dress covered with a thousand jewels. Well—

PET. Don't stop here. Did he kill her?

BLAZ. Awkward corners are turned in the drama now by a steam-curtain, and this is a deuced awkward one. Theoretically, you know, an Englishman never lifts his hand against a woman—

JACK (interrupting). Unless she is his wife—

PET. When he uses his feet, so that don't count. Pardon us, Lord Blazonberrie.

BLAZ. Don't mention it. As I say, the steam-curtain covers a multitude of sins, and up ours goes. See it? (Waves his hands.) On it goes, growing pinker every instant, until the orchestra strikes up, "See the conquering hero comes !" and *voila!* a new scene appears—England again. Sir Guy greets his happy tenantry once more, and settles down to enjoy—the proceeds of—his virtuous career.

PET. But where does the necklace come in ?

BLAZ. It was one of the rewards of his virtue.

PET. Good men flourish like Christmas-trees in India, don't they ?

BLAZ. Not when they are handicapped by a dying woman's curse, as Sir Guy was.

JACK. Give us the curse.

BLAZ. Gladly.

> "Tell my tale of woe to four,
> Disasters follow by the score."

So the family doggerel goes, and numerous unpleasant coincidences back it up. The Ranee objected to gossip evidently.

PET. But we are only four now ! (*Jumps up.*) Gracious ! Just fancy !

DUCHESS. Only four ? Where are Dick and Tulu ?

JACK. They slipped away before Blazon-berrie began.

DUCHESS. How unfortunate! Blazonberrie, why were you so careless?

BLAZ. Nonsense! Have in the lights and put the beastly thing away. Who cares for such things now?

DUCHESS. Well, it cannot be helped. Put it away.

JACK. May I have one more look?

BLAZ. Certainly. (*Hands it to him.*)

JACK (*coming down* F.). The exact thing for my East Indian story. (*Examines it.*)

PET. Does anything happen to Jack and I, or is it a strictly Blazonberrie picnic?

BLAZ. I bear the brunt as narrator, and you all come in for second places. Shall we have a game of billiards, and so return to the nineteenth century?

PET. By all means. I feel really creepy. Come and score, Jack. Duchess, come and see me wipe up the floor with Lord Blazonberrie. (*Exit*, C. E., *with* BLAZ.)

DUCHESS. Wipe up the floor!

JACK. Another American atrocity, Duchess. Shall we join them?

DUCHESS. First I must ask your assistance in locking these away. Sorry to bore you, but I cannot trust servants in this case.

JACK. Charmed to be of service, I assure you. Where does this fascinating thing go, Duchess?

DUCHESS. In the bottom, well out of sight. I detest it.

JACK. Then you will not wear it to the masquerade to-morrow?

DUCHESS. No; I very seldom wear it. Put it in now, if you please.

(JACK *lays necklace in box,* DUCHESS *puts in trays.*)

DUCHESS. Thanks. Now, Mr. Ryder—you are a Yankee—I have one of your country-men's safes in this room. Look about, and guess where it is.

JACK (*aside*). It's an awful death to die! (*Aloud.*) I cannot imagine, Duchess. In the wainscot?

DUCHESS (*crossing to desk*). No; here, un-der this etching. Is it not clever? I will open it. The word was Toedmag. T-o-e-d-m-a-g, and our simple little etching swings out, revealing the patent American fire-proof safe.

13

JACK (*handing her jewel-box*). And the word is changed every time?

DUCHESS. Yes. This time you shall select it.

JACK. How would Petrolia do?

(BLAZONBERRIE *enters*, C.; *stands listening.*)

DUCHESS. Admirable! (*Places box in safe; closes it.*) P-e-t-r-o-l-i-a. Now, Mr. Ryder, not even Blazonberrie shall know the secret.

JACK. I appreciate your confidence, Duchess. Shall we join the others?

(BLAZONBERRIE *drops curtain; retires.*)

DUCHESS. Dick will be here almost immediately, to take that absurd picture. Thank fortune, Blazonberrie never has any wearing fads. He is such a *dear* fellow.

JACK (*absent-mindedly*). I have always heard he was very expensive. Pardon me, I was not attending.

DUCHESS. Do not mention it. By-the-bye, I want your opinion on an old book I picked up at auction. It is in here. Come! (*Exit*, L.)

JACK. Confound her old book! I wonder what Petrolia is doing.

DUCHESS (*outside*). I am waiting, Mr. Ryder.

JACK. Coming, Duchess.   (*Exit*, L.)

(*Enter* TULU *and* DICK, C.)

TULU. Don't be a goose and spoil everything, Mr. Dick.

DICK. But it's not the correct thing.   A *man* should never play upon a woman's weakness.

TULU (*laughing*). A man! Why, you're nothing but a boy—an infant, without a mustache.

DICK. I've three, nearly four years the advantage of you, Miss Tulu.

TULU. Pooh! it's brains that count, not years.   Our boys at home can give you points every time. (*Sits on sofa.*) However, *be* hateful! Petrolia has played no end of jokes on you, and says you're the freshest thing she ever saw.   So there!

DICK. Oh, she did! She had better look in the glass.   I am fresh, am I?   Very good, then I am with you.   Where is it?

TULU. It?

DICK. The blamed mouse.

TULU. Keep your temper, little boy. (*Takes candy mouse from her pocket.*) Here's the blamed mouse. (*Dangles it by tail.*) Isn't it natural?

DICK. No end. And will your sister yell when she sees it?

TULU. Yell! Well, I guess. Smithy is so awfully silly. She'll make a perfect idiot of herself, and when she's quite through we'll say, " Why, it's only chocolate !"

DICK. That's the idea! and I will add, "You are the freshest thing I ever saw." That will crush her. (*Voices outside.*)

TULU. Remember the cue: " We're all ready."

DICK. Do it the first thing. (*Runs to camera.*)

(*Enter* BLAZONBERRIE *and* PETROLIA, C., DUCH-ESS *and* JACK, L.)

PET. Duchess, the curse begins to work. I have promised Mr. Chetwyn to sit for him until he gets a picture. Fancy! By-and-by I shall be known as—the plate-smasher.

DUCHESS. I am grieved that Dick should bore you, Miss Seersucker.

JACK. My cousin jests. She is incapable of being serious about anything.

PET. Thanks.

DICK. Some of her jokes go a long way.

PET. Yes; they came over three thousand miles with me.

TULU. But other people can joke as well, even if they are young.

PET. Gracious! who pickled the party while I was out? Lord Blazonberrie, let us pose as two cherubim on the tête-à-tête, and show the beauty of a sweet temper. (*Goes to tête-à-tête; sits.*)

BLAZ. (*following*). Yes, teach 'em a lesson. (*Sits by her.*)

DUCHESS (*going to chair, R. F.*). Mr. Ryder, will you join me? (*Sits.*)

JACK (*crossing to her*). With the greatest pleasure. (*Sits glaring at* PET., *who is flirting with* BLAZ.)

TULU. I'll be in the background. (*Steals behind* PET., *pins mouse on her skirt.*)

DICK. All ready?

TULU. We're all ready. (*Winks to* DICK.)

DICK. Very good. Jove! Miss Seersucker, is that a mouse crawling up your skirt?

PET. A mouse on me! Take it off!
Quick! (*Jumps on tête-à-tête, screams.*) Do
catch it! Oh! oh!

BLAZ. (*hunting on floor*). I don't see it.

JACK (*rushing to* PET.). Keep cool, Petrolia,
I'll get it.

PET. Hurry! hurry! Jack, take the horrid thing away!

DUCHESS (*rising*). Atrocious! What a
scene!

(TULU and DICK *laugh uproariously.*)

PET. It touched my hand! Oh, Jack,
why are you so slow?

BLAZ. I don't see it. (*Hunts under table.*)

JACK. Ah, I've got you! (*Seizes mouse,
holds it up.*) Why, it's only chocolate. See,
Petrolia.

TULU. Only chocolate! Ha! ha! ha!

DICK. Who's fresh now? Ha! ha! ha!

PET. Only chocolate? Duchess, pardon
me, but I've such a horror of mice. Whose
idea was it? Tulu!

DICK (*promptly*). I am the culprit, Miss

Seersucker. I only intended a little fun—a little revenge—

Pet. And had a great deal. Then I owe you one, Mr. Chetwyn. And I always pay my debts—always.

TABLEAU.

PET.   JACK.

TULU.   BLAZ.

DUCHESS.   DICK.

CURTAIN.

ACT II.

(*Same scene, lamps lighted;* DUCHESS, PETRO-LIA, *and* TULU *enter in evening dress.*)

DUCHESS. So you have society in the States? Amazing!

TULU. You bet we have society!

PET. Tulu! (*Goes to fire.*)

TULU. You can't bulldoze me, Smithy. Besides, the Duchess spoke to me.

DUCHESS. Indeed, I did not. (*Sits by table.*) Were you my child you would be in the school-room.

Tulu. Thank goodness, I'm not your child. (*Flings herself on sofa, looks over picture-book.*)

Duchess. Miss Seersucker, Dick tells me there is a truly correct and English style of living among your "Four Hundred"—not that I know what they are—but how do the rest of the fifty million live? For instance, how do you dine *en famille?*

Pet. (*coming forward*). How do we dine? Well; I remember a dinner we gave Mr. Chetwyn last summer. First course, fried ham—

Duchess. Very original. Was it served before or after soup?

Tulu. The Seersuckers never get in the soup, Duchess.

Duchess. Never get in! Why, who does?

Tulu. Blazonberrie is in it—

Pet. Tulu! More slang, Duchess. It means the reverse of in the swim—

Tulu. It does not. It means—

Pet. Tulu! (*Very fast.*) Next course, trout, olives, baked potatoes, jam, pickles, sardines, crackers, and fried coffee—at least, it was made in the frying-pan.

Duchess. Pray how was this served?

PET. *A la Russe*, on tin pie-plates.

DUCHESS. Did all these things go well together?

PET. Everything *goes* in the Adirondacks.

DUCHESS. Ah, now I see. The Adirondacks are a suburb of New York City, are they not?

TULU. What jolly geography!

PET. Yes, Duchess.

DUCHESS. And this was before your father —er—hit oil.

TULU. *Hit* oil! Ha! ha! ha! She means *struck*, Smithy.

DUCHESS. I see no difference.

PET. Papa struck oil before I was born, Duchess; hence my idiotic name. Petroleum—Petrolia. See?

DUCHESS (*condescendingly*). I like your name exceedingly, Miss Seersucker; it is so distinctive. Many daughters are named after their fathers' professions in the States, are they not?

PET. As there is not apt to be any daughter before there is a profession, they are.

DUCHESS. How interesting! Give me a few specimens.

PET. (*winks to* TULU). Certainly.   There's Julia Vanderbilt: father a carpenter named Vander, built; Jennie Rockafeller: mother a nurse, rocked many a feller; Jemima Hodson: father carried a hod; Mary—er—well, so on; not to mention Gloviana, Sopiana, Drygoodsia, and Drugolia.

TULU (*aside*). Can't she just reel them off!

DUCHESS. It is like the Norse formation of names.   Peculiarly suited to a people without rank, traditions, or ancestors.

PET. We were not incubated!   (*Rises.*)

DUCHESS (*soothingly*). No, no; but I understand grandfathers are best ignored in the States, and every one starts on the basis that the child is father of the man.

PET. Indeed we don't.   We are mighty proud of the men who made our blooming young republic, and wouldn't swap one of them for any number of your gone-to-seed aristocracy.

DUCHESS. Gone to seed!   (*Rises.*)

PET. (*walking about*). Yes.   Your great families were built up by men of the people, men with brains, and are about to be extinguished by a set of vapid fops—

DUCHESS. Atrocious!

TULU (*throwing book on floor*). Go it, Smithy!

PET. Yes; your family trees boast only withered sprouts — bargain - counter dukes, shop - worn earls, and mildewed lords, who follow their titles into the American market like tin kettles tied to a dog's tail.

DUCHESS (*going to door*). Perhaps you would do well to reserve your scorn until one of these same titles is offered you, Miss Seersucker.

TULU. Oh, rats! She's refused six lords, one—

PET. Tulu!

DUCHESS. I cannot listen; I have recollected an important letter. Atrocious! (*Exit*, c.)

TULU (*running to door*). And a baronet. So there!

PET. (*putting hand over her mouth*). Tulu, please be quiet.

TULU. Well, you did.

PET. (*laughing*). Tulu, you never say such horrid things at home.

TULU. No more do you. You set me a very bad example.

PET. I know it.   But it is such fun to see the Duchess's eyes.

TULU. Isn't it?   And it's so dull here. I say, Petrolia, are you going to marry Blazonberrie?

PET. (*sitting on tête-à-tête*). What do you advise?

TULU. I s'pose it would be fun to be Lady Blazonberrie now, and a duchess by-and-by, but Jack is nicer.

PET. I should think so!

TULU. And Blazonberrie is as cross as a bear mornings.   He swears at his valet.   Mr. Dick is so much jollier he ought to be a lord.

PET. He is a nuisance, and I owe him one.

TULU. I think he is perfectly sweet.

PET. He is very selfish.   Just think, Tulu, he has never let you take one picture.   Just as though you were a baby.

TULU. Yes, and I know I could do it as well as he does.

PET. You could not well do it worse. (*Draws her to her.*)   Wouldn't it be fun to take one on the sly, dear?

TULU. *Dear!*   What do you want?

PET. Only a little revenge. He made me appear a perfect fool, you know.

TULU. Well, I'm in it.

PET. That's a dear child. (*Hugs her.*) You know the camera is all ready for a flash-light picture.

TULU. Yep.

PET. Very good. After coffee is served, and we have all gone to the music-room, you wait behind. Turn out the light. Hide behind the curtain with the bulb in your hand. I will send Mr. Chetwyn back for my handkerchief. The instant he is in the door, give a horrible groan and squeeze the bulb. You can't miss him, and of course he will have his mouth open.

TULU. I'll groan so. (*Groans.*) Wouldn't that make your flesh just creep?

PET. Yes, indeed. And to-morrow you can have Saunders finish it quietly, and then show it to everybody.

TULU. Mr. Dick will be just hopping.

(*Enter JACK, C.*)

JACK. Run away, Tulu, like a good child.

TULU. I'm not a child; I'm fifteen, and I

don't want to hear your old secret. (*Walks very slowly to door.*) 'Tisn't much of a secret. You're going to make love to Petrolia, like all the rest. (*Exit,* L.)

PET. What is the matter, Jack?

JACK. You.

PET. What have I did?

JACK. Do be serious, Petrolia, I want to speak to you.

PET. Well, you seem to be talking.

JACK. You know what I mean.

PET. That is what Blazonberrie constantly says.

JACK. Confound him!

PET. Was it of this you wished to speak?

JACK. No. (*Walks about.*) Petrolia, it is, of course, not my affair, but I wish you would leave these insolent people, who regard you as a speculation and a curiosity. I am continually irritated by the Duchess's tone of patronage.

PET. Are you? I enjoy our battles immensely, and her patronage does not injure me.

JACK. I think it does, Petrolia. I think that when a beautiful, accomplished, fascinating girl like you puts herself in the position of being "sent on approval," as it were, she is injured.

PET. But it is the other way. Blazonberrie is "on approval." And of course, Jack, no true American could reject a title.

JACK. You could.

PET. I am not sure. (*Rises.*) If papa buys me Blazonberrie, think how I can stamp on the women who have hesitated to receive "Old Bob's" daughter. (*Crosses to* R.)

JACK (*following*). What have these women to do with your real happiness, Petrolia?

PET. Not much. Oh, Jack! sometimes I wish papa had never made his fortune. (*They walk slowly to* C., *stand in front of tête-à-tête.*)

JACK. I often wish that.

PET. Do you remember the larks we had at Cobbsville? The dances in the school-house, and the everlasting pink gingham gown I wore?

JACK. You never wear anything half so sweet now. One is afraid to touch you for fear of rumpling some folds or biases.

PET. I recollect one who was afraid to touch me then, Master Jack. Do you remem-

ber the night you kissed me behind the door,
and I walked home on the fence, with you
following in the moonlight, and wouldn't
speak to you? (*They sit on tête-à-tête.*)

JACK. Yes; and I remember calling with
a basket of apples and an apology the next
morning, and you forgave me.

PET. Yes; and taught you to waltz out in
the barn. (*Laughs.*) Oh, Jack! shall you
ever forget the quarrel we had because I said
Tommy Hicks had a handsome nose?

JACK. No; nor how I flattened his handsome nose. Dear old days! (*Sighs.*)

PET. Dear, dear old days! (*Sighs.*) What
a pity that "youth's sweet-scented manuscript
must close," as Khayam says.

JACK. Why need it? Petrolia, you have
just said your happiest days were those in
which you had no money. And they were.
Money brings cares, social obligations, heart-
burnings in its train. It cannot buy happiness, or love such as I offer you. My love
has never swerved since we were children
playing together. I—

PET. Well, Jack?

JACK (*taking her hand*). Petrolia, would

you—oh, were it not for your money I would tell you of the fond dreams I have had of a little home, where you should reign supreme. Were it not for that miserable fortune, I would offer you the devotion of a lifetime. But, pshaw! (*Rises, walks about.*) I am poor, always shall be. Authorship brings no golden reward — and I am absurd with my talk of love. Love is for the rich nowadays.

PET. I am sorry, because then I never shall have any.

JACK. You! Why, your fortune is my stumbling-block.

PET. Yes, now. But, you see, Jack, papa said—he said, you know—he said—

JACK (*rushing to her*). Yes, Petrolia—he said—

PET. He said if I was such—a—a darned fool as to prefer you to an English lord, I might marry you and live on love, for he'd never give me a cent.

JACK. And would you give it up for me?

PET. I—

DICK (*outside*). Tulu!

JACK. Chetwyn.

14

(DICK *enters*, C.)

PET. Yes. Get rid of the tiresome boy, and I'll come back in ten minutes. (*Exit*, L.)

DICK (*coming forward*). Hope I do not interrupt, Ryder.

JACK. I thought you were in the billiard-room.

DICK (*seating himself on desk*). I was, but I am detachable and peripatetic.

JACK. Ah! very good, very good. Um—er—just excuse me a moment. (*Aside.*) I must find Petrolia. (*Exit*, L.)

DICK (*imitating*). Very good — um — er — just excuse me a moment. Now I wonder if ever I will be so tangled up over any girl. And to think they are dead spoons on each other, and I never knew it! "Get rid of that tiresome boy," says she, "and I'll be back in a moment." Werry well; you shall finish your proposal quite comfortable for all me. (*Jumps down from desk.*) Jupiter! what a jolly row Aunt Hildegarde will kick up when she finds it out! I wish I could have her in at the finish and take her picture. (*Laughs.*) It's too good to be lost, and part of it shall be a picture—not necessarily for publication, but to pay Miss Petrolia for calling me a tiresome boy. (*Moves camera so it takes in tête-à-tête.*) There! Of course they will sit on the tête-à-tête; that's what they are made for—proposals. Ought to be called pop-cushions. (*Lays bulb in front of seat.*) There you are, convenient to Ryder's foot. When he starts up, crying, "Darling, I love you!" he steps on my little friend, and a charming picture is caught just as she tumbles into his arms—so. (*Falls on seat.*) I hope Ryder will have the decency to keep on his own side. I fancy it will be all right, for she'll jump or wiggle—they all do—and skip back, with a coy shriek—so—and off goes the picture. If I were only a boy again I'd hide behind the curtain; as I cannot, I must trust to luck. Now for the light. (*Turns down lamp. Stage dark.*) Jove! where's the door? Ow! there I go again! Well, bones are cheap. Ah, here I am. (*Exit, c.*)

(*Enter* TULU, L.)

TULU (*feeling her way*). Whatever is the matter? Oh, I s'pose this is more of the

Duchess's economy. Oh no; Mr. Dick is going to take a picture. Well, he sha'n't spoil my joke on him. I'll hide on the sofa, and interfere somehow. My! Gracious! Oh! Ah! I guess I broke my ankle that time. (*Hobbles to sofa.*) I never was so bored. I never did see such a poky old house. I believe Mr. Dick is coming.

(*Enter* BLAZONBERRIE, C.)

BLAZ. What the dickens— Anybody here?

TULU. Only me.

BLAZ. Who is "me?" Ah, Miss Seersucker! I should know your charming voice anywhere.

TULU. Should you really? (*Aside.*) He takes me for Petrolia. What a lark!

BLAZ. Why is it dark?

TULU. My head aches fearfully, so I turned the lights down, and am trying to compose myself.

BLAZ. I'm no end sorry. May I talk to you? Where are you?

TULU. On the sofa. Don't break your shins over the chairs.

BLAZ. (*tumbling over chair*). Da—ahem!

ahem! May I sit by you, Miss Seer-sucker?

TULU (*laughing*). I guess so.

BLAZ. Your voice sounds so like Tulu's in the dark.

TULU (*giggling*). That's queer.

BLAZ. Shall I turn up the light just a bit?

TULU. No, no! My head is awful! (*Groans.*)

BLAZ. Jove! It's too bad. Perhaps I bore you.

TULU. *You* could *never* bore *me*, Lord Blazonberrie.

BLAZ. Do you mean that? You're such a one for chaff, a fellow never knows.

TULU. Oh, I meant that.

BLAZ. Miss Seersucker—Petrolia! The—er—darkness gives me courage to say—what I have tried to ever since you came—only you have bluffed me off.

TULU. No, I didn't.

BLAZ. But you seemed to. And a fellow loaded with debts and so forth, has not got much to offer.

TULU. I have enough for two. (*Giggles.*)

Blaz. If you are making game of me, I am silent.

Tulu. I am hysterical, that's all.

Blaz. Well, then, to cut it short, will you be my wife?

Tulu. I don't exactly know. The Duchess is a corker for a mother-in-law.

Blaz. She will retire to her dower house.

Tulu. That's so. It certainly would be slick to be Lady Blazonberrie.

Blaz. Be what?

Tulu. Slick. *Smooth*, you know. Still, I hardly know what to say.

Blaz. Are you engaged to Ryder?

Tulu. That's what gets me. I don't know.

Blaz. Don't know!

Tulu. No. (*Rushes off*, l.)

Blaz. I say! Look here, you know. (*Turns up light.*) Gone! Now, is this American coquetry or unadulterated idiocy? Don't know whether she's engaged or not! I will be obliged if she will find out, for my affairs are coming to a crisis. Smash is the word unless money comes from somewhere. (*Walks up and down*). Going to smash for

twenty thousand pounds, and over six times
that amount over there (*points to sofa*), tied
up by that beastly entail. The entail business is played out. What's this? (*Picks up
amulet.*) Ryder's fetish. Let him hunt for
it if he wants it. (*Throws amulet down.*)
And he, with his priggish airs, stands between me and two hundred thousand pounds
sterling and a wife who thinks it would be
slick—no, *smooth*—to be Lady Blazonberrie.
Good Gad! what an ornament to the peer-
age! However, she's a well-gilded pill, and
I never heard her out before in such howling
bad form as she was to-night.

(*Enter* PETROLIA, C. E.)

PET. Jack! Pardon me, Lord Blazonberrie; I thought my cousin was here. Have
you seen him?

BLAZ. No; he has not been here since you
left. I have waited, and am waiting, for my
answer. How could you run away?

PET. How could I run away? (*Comes forward.*)

BLAZ. Yes, and leave me in such—such—
er—harrowing uncertainty?

PET. I?

BLAZ. If it were not you, who was it?

PET. (*bewidlered*). If it were not I, who was
it?

BLAZ. (*impatiently*). That is what I said.

PET. Ah, it is an English joke.

BLAZ. More in the American style, I fancy.
First, you say it will be slick—smooth—to be
Lady Blazonberrie; secondly, that you do
not know whether you are engaged to Ryder
or not.   How do you explain that?

PET. When did I say all this?

BLAZ. Not five minutes ago; and, I say,
how do you explain it?

PET. I don't.   I can't.   I am all in the
dark.

BLAZ. Well, you are a very different young
lady in the dark, I assure you.   I wish I had
not turned up the light.

PET. Oh, I see!   All this happened in the
dark.

BLAZ. I should think you might recollect
that.

PET. (*aside*). This is Tulu's mischief!
(*Aloud.*) You are making a vastly serious
matter of this.

BLAZ. It is serious. I must know if you are engaged to Ryder.

PET. I deny your right to question me.

BLAZ. I have a right to know if I am being misled.

PET. I am not misleading you.

BLAZ. (*sitting by her*). Then you love me! You will be my wife!

PET. Do you love me, Lord Blazonberrie?

(JACK *appears in door*, c.)

BLAZ. I am not a sentimental fellow, but I think you are no end jolly, and I want you to be my wife.

(JACK *makes gesture of despair, disappears.*)

PET. Exactly. And were there no question of settlements, I am the ideal wife you would select to do the honors of your house?

BLAZ. Well—I—

PET. (*rising*). You answer yourself. You regard me as a creature quite outside the pale of civilization, a vulgar Philistine, bad form in every sense of the word, and only to be tolerated for the money I bring. Pardon me if I speak too frankly, but I do not think you offer me a fair equivalent.

BLAZ. Yet you seemed to like the prospect of being a duchess.   (*Rises, walks about.*)

PET. I own I was dazzled.   There was a time when it seemed quite a splendid position, but now I realize it is a paltry affair.

BLAZ. I see.   Ryder steps between us.

PET. He has nothing to do with the case.

BLAZ. I heard nothing of this virtuous contempt for rank until he appeared.   Well, I accept my defeat.   He is a nice enough fellow, but I doubt if he is quite the hero you imagine him.

PET. He is at least incapable of the meanness of—of—

BLAZ. Marrying for money?   Don't balk at the word.   So am I.   I couldn't marry you without it, but, believe me, Miss Seersucker, were you less fascinating than you are, even your fortune would not tempt me.

PET. Oh, Lord Blazonberrie, I hope you do not really care for me.

BLAZ. Care!

PET. Say no more.   Let us forget this wretched scene.   I do not love you, but I feel more real friendship for you than I could ever have fancied possible. (*Gives him her hand.*)

BLAZ. (*kissing her hand*). Friendship is cold comfort, but I accept it. And I shall never give you up—never!

PET. Oh, I must not stay. Think no more of me, Lord Blazonberrie, I beg of you. (*Exit*, L.)

BLAZ. (*coming down* F.). That was a neat recover, I think. Why the dickens did I balk so over telling her I loved her, in the first place? I fancy it was that scene in the dark. With that fresh in my mind I really could not tell her she was an ideal duchess. However, I patched it up neatly. She is full of sympathy for my love-lorn state, and that's a distinct move. Now, could I but overturn her little hero from his pedestal, she is mine. How to do it—that's the question.

(*Enter* ROBINSON, C.)

ROB. (*handing him letter*). A letter, my lord. Boy from the Blue Cow, waiting for a hanser.

BLAZ. (*tearing letter open*). Rosenthal's

writing ! (*Reads, crumples letter.*) Confound
it !

ROB. (*aside*). A dun.

BLAZ. (*writes note at desk, turns to* ROB.).
Here, give this to the boy. What are you
staring at ?

ROB. Nothing, my lord.

BLAZ. You lie. You were staring at me.

ROB. Yes, my lord.

BLAZ. Leave the room.

ROB. Yes, my lord. (*Aside.*) Hit was a
dun. (*Exit,* c.)

BLAZ. (*coming down* F., *reading letter*). " Let
me call your lordship's attention to the fact
that your lordship's bill for twenty thousand
pounds comes due to-morrow, and must be
taken up. Have spoken to my principal as
you desired, and he says he can't possibly
renew even for one month. Shall remain at
the inn until ten o'clock to-morrow, when, if
I neither see nor hear from your lordship, will
be obliged to come up to the castle. Trusting your lordship will see the necessity of
giving this your immediate attention, I remain, your lordship's humble servant, A. Rosenthal. **At the Blue Cow.** December

20th." (*Crushes letter in his hand.*) Damn
his smooth impudence! Come up here and
make a scene, will he? How the deuce can
I raise twenty thousand pounds? Don't he
know that there's not a Jew in London ready
to advance me another sov.? And the Duke
is drained dry. By Jove, there never was
such an unfortunate fellow as I! The small-
est bet I can make on a horse breaks his
wind or his leg; while anything large brings
battle, murder, and sudden death to horse
and jockey both. Then this chit of a girl
gets up on her ear just as I counted on her
fortune to mend my own. Were I engaged
to her, Rosenthal would wait. But how to
manage it, how to manage it? (*Exit,* L.)

(*Enter* JACK, C.)

JACK. Not here, of course. After the
touching scene I interrupted, how could I expect it? And yet I did. I did. (*Comes
forward, sits,* C.) I should have known she
could not refuse his title, but I loved her and
believed in her. "Do you love me?" she
asked, and doubtless he swore he did. He's
just the style of fellow women admire, hand-

some, dull, and soft in his manner. Latent
strength, they call it, when it's only repressed
idiocy. Pshaw! I won't think of it. She
shall never know how deep a wound she has
inflicted. I will leave to-morrow; that I am
resolved on.

(*Enter* DICK, L.)

DICK (*aside*). *He's* here. I'll get the light
out, and send her. (*Aloud.*) Are you asleep,
Ryder?

JACK (*turning*). Ah, Chetwyn! I was won-
dering where everybody was.

DICK (*sitting* L. F.). I say, what a jolly lot
we are! all straying about like Banshees, except my revered aunt, who has retired with a
—pain in her temper. That's chronic with
her. Maybe you have one yourself.

JACK. No; I was meditating.

DICK. It seems to take a good deal out of
you. (*Winks.*) Cheer up. She will be here
directly.

JACK. The Duchess?

DICK. Not much. Your charming cousin,
Miss Seersucker. She asked me where you
were, and I said in here, so says she—er—

"Run in and tell him I am coming," and I
ran.

JACK (*stiffly*). You are most obliging.

DICK. Don't mention it. . (*Aside.*) Now
for the light. (*Aloud.*) What ails the light?
(*Fumbles with lamp.*) It seems to — ugh!
ah!—what a beast of a lamp!

JACK. It burns well enough. You're turning it out.

DICK. Not a bit of it. (*Turns it out.
Stage dark.*) Jove! what a fool of a lamp!

JACK. I knew you'd do it. I'll fetch a
match.

DICK. No, no! Miss Petrolia will miss
you. I'll fetch one. Where are you?

JACK. Sitting on the tête-à-tête.

DICK. That's all right. I'll be back in an
instant. (*Exit*, c.)

JACK. So she is coming to smooth me
down again. For once she will find me in-
flexible. (*Pause.*) Why don't that idiot of
a boy come back? (*Pause.*) Well, I am
soft! Master Dick is playing one of his
charming jokes on me. I knew he was fool-
ing about the lamp. I'll go to my room and
pack. Where is the door? Ah! here. So

ends your joke, Master Dick. (*Runs into* Rob., *entering* c. e.)

Rob. Beg parding.

Jack. No matter. (*Goes off,* c.)

Rob. That was the Hamerican. Wothever was 'e a-doing hall halone hin the dark? (*Lights lamp.*)

(*Enter* Petrolia *and* Tulu, l.)

Pet. Robinson, where is the Duchess?

Rob. 'Er ladyship 'ave retired to 'er room, Miss Seersucker, hand begs you will hexcuse 'er for the rest of the hevening, has she is very much hindispoged.

Pet. Is it anything serious, Robinson?

Rob. Nothing serious, miss.

Tulu. She's boiling mad, Petrolia.

Pet. Tulu!

Rob. Do you require hanything, miss?

Pet. No. You may go.

(Robinson *goes off,* c.)

Tulu. You'll make a jolly duchess, Petrolia. You say "You may go" exactly like your mother-in-law. I'm glad she is ill;

maybe she won't get in such a jolly wax for nothing again.

PET. It is another bit of insolence.

TULU. Who cares? Come on in the billiard-room; Dick and Blazonberrie are there, and I'll fetch Jack. Come on.

PET. Are you crazy, Tulu? We can't stay down without our hostess and chaperon, and entertain a party of young men—at least, not in England.

TULU. We can't go to bed at ten o'clock.

PET. We must go up to my sitting-room and read. Come, Tulu, and we will leave as soon as we can possibly find an excuse.

TULU. But my joke on Dick! Oh, Smithy!

PET. That will keep. Please come, Tulu.

TULU. Well, you go, and I will follow.

PET. (*laughing*). Sure 'nuff?

TULU. Sure 'nuff. Skip, Smithy.

PET. Don't be long. (*Exit*, c.)

TULU. I sha'n't go until I have taken Mr. Dick's picture. He will have to pass through here to the smoking-room. (*Arranges camera by tea-table so it takes in c. e.*) There! that ought to get him. (*Picks up bulb.*) Now

15

for the light. (*Turns out light. Stage dark.*)
I'll get behind the table. (*Pause.*)   My! it's
awful hot here, and I'm getting sleepy.   I
wish Mr. Dick would hurry. (*Yawns.*)   I'm
so—sleepy. (*Pause.*)

(BLAZONBERRIE *enters,* C.)

BLAZ. All dark again.   So much the better.   Jove! how my heart thumps!   I am
only robbing myself.   The jewels are mine
—or will be—and the entail can go to the
deuce. (*Soft music until end of scene.*)   The
Duchess never wears the thing, so it will not
be missed; or if it is—*I do not know the
combination.* (*Lights match, goes to desk.*)
What did I step on? (*Stoops down.*)   Ryder's amulet again.   Stay there!   Should the
worst come, you are circumstantial evidence.
(*Lights match, turns handle of safe.*)   P-e-
t-r-o-l-i-a, and out you come. (*Takes out Ranee's necklace, replaces jewel-box, closes safe
by light of matches.   Goes to* C. E.)

TULU (*whispering*).   Mr. Dick is here;
now, then! (*Squeezes bulb.   Flash shows
BLAZ. by* C. E., *his hand raised, holding necklace.*)

BLAZ. A light! Some one coming! (*Rush-es off.*)

TULU. I forgot to groan. (*Goes to camera.*)

TABLEAU.

TULU *taking out plate.*

CURTAIN.

(*The flash can be imitated by quickly uncovering white light in* L. E., *so it strikes full on* BLAZONBERRIE.)

ACT III.

Same scene; morning; music. Curtain rises on BLAZONBERRIE *and* PETROLIA, JACK *and* TULU, *dancing gavotte, or fancy dance;* DICK *sitting on table,* L., *playing on comb. They dance one measure, then music grows fainter, so they talk while dancing.*

DICK. You will be belles of the ball, special ly Tulu, who dances like a pantomime fairy.

TULU. Yes, I can dance. Jack, I wish you would not look so dismal.

JACK. I'm as jolly as a sand-boy. Here we go—forward, back, and round again.

BLAZ. Miss Seersucker, may we not know what character you take in the masquerade to-night?

PET. That is a secret between the Duchess and I.

DICK. I bet I know.

TULU. I bet you don't. Why, even I don't.

JACK. You might tell me, Petrolia; I shall not be here to-night.

PET. Not be here? (*Stops dancing.*)

TULU. Not be here? After rehearsing the dance, and getting your costume! Oh, Jack!

DICK. It will spoil the whole thing.

BLAZ. Is not this rather sudden, Mr. Ryder?

JACK. You do not object, I suppose, Lord Blazonberrie?

BLAZ. Not at all.

PET. How mysterious! (*Goes to fire with* BLAZ.)

DICK (*going to* JACK). I say, old fellow, you must not desert us.

TULU (*taking his hand*). Please stay, Jack.

(DUCHESS *enters*, C.)

JACK. I must go, Tulu. Duty calls me.

TULU. Then I think you are perfectly hateful. But I don't care! I've got something to attend to—something important. Don't you wish you knew, Master Dick?

DICK. I suppose you are going to wash your new puppy.

TULU. A puppy is in it. (*Laughs.*) You'll know in about ten minutes. (*Runs off*, L.)

DUCHESS (*advancing*). Did I hear you say you were going to leave us, Mr. Ryder?

JACK. I regret to say I must, Duchess.

DUCHESS. Must?

DICK. There's thunder in the air. (*Crosses to* R.)

JACK. Yes—business in London, some work overdue—in short, I must take the 11.10 mail up.

DUCHESS. But your departure breaks up the party to the masquerade. I do not understand why you must do that. The mail is not here, no telegrams have arrived. It must be a mere caprice.

JACK. Call it so if you please, Duchess, but I cannot remain.

DUCHESS. Very good. (*Turns her back.*) Miss Seersucker, Wiggins is ready for you. I will get the necklace, and we will try the effect.

PET. Thanks, Duchess ; I am quite ready.

BLAZ. What is the costume, mother ?

DUCHESS (*going to safe*). Has not Miss Seersucker told you ? She is to be the Ranee, and wear the necklace.

BLAZ. Wear the Ranee's necklace ! Jove ! —er—what a jolly idea ! (*Comes down* F. *Aside.*) It has come. It is now a toss-up between Ryder and me. One of us goes to the wall, and, by Jove ! it shall not be me. (*To* PET.) You could not have made a more becoming or, to me, a more flattering choice.

PET. Flattering ! Why, I thought, on the contrary—ah, I beg your pardon, Lord Blazonberrie.

JACK (*aside*). It is evidently all settled. I must take myself off. Duchess, I have the honor to thank you for your kind hospitality, and to wish you good-bye.

DUCHESS. Pardon me for detaining you,

but I have forgotten the combination. Usually I write the word in my note-book. This time I trusted to your memory.

JACK. Permit me to assist you. (*Unlocks safe, hands* DUCHESS *jewel-box. She takes out tray, gives box back.*)

DUCHESS. One moment more. Will you hold this tray while I— Great heavens! I —oh! great heavens! What shall I do? (*All rush to her.*)

PET. Oh, what is the matter?

DUCHESS. We are robbed! Blazonberrie, the Ranee's necklace is gone!

JACK. The Ranee's necklace?

PET. The Ranee's necklace?

JACK. Why, I saw you put it there myself.

DICK (*examining tray*). It is gone, no denying it.

BLAZ. Impossible! Diamonds do not exhale. There must be some mistake, some stupidity. Who knew the combination?

DUCHESS. Why, only Mr. Ryder and I.

JACK. Yes, only the Duchess and myself.

BLAZ. (*starts*). Only! Ah!

DICK. What ails you?

BLAZ. Nothing.

JACK. And I told no one.

DUCHESS. Nor I.

BLAZ. (*starts again*). Why, that looks—Oh, nonsense !

DUCHESS. Looks ? Looks what ? Why do you not finish your sentence ? (*Pause.*) I insist.

BLAZ. (*affecting to lower his voice*). Do you not see ? It is impossible, incredible ! I am host in my own house, not a detective.

DUCHESS. Not a detective, you mean ?

BLAZ. (*glancing at Ryder*). That it is best to say no more. The house of Toedmag can better afford to pocket its loss than to—

DICK. Oh ! By Jove ! Blazonberrie, you don't mean—

JACK (*stepping forward*). Perhaps Lord Blazonberrie will kindly explain what he does mean.

BLAZ. (*haughtily*). I have said nothing, sir !

PET. But you *look* volumes.

DUCHESS. Look ! Well he may. I see it all ! No one but Mr. Ryder and myself knew the combination. He thought I should not wear the necklace. He asks me most particularly about it. He arranges to be called away by business just remembered; and supposed the loss will not be discovered until 'he has made his escape. Mr. Ryder, give me my necklace! Blazonberrie, secure the doors and summon the police.

PET. Duchess, you dare to say — you mean?

BLAZ. My dear Miss Seersucker, you will, I am sure, pardon the Duchess who is in a fearfully excited condition.

TULU (*outside*). Mr. Dick! Mr. Dick!

DICK. Oh! I say, Miss Seersucker, shall I head off poor little Tulu? Send her off to Saunders?

PET. Yes, do. She is so excitable.

(*Exit* DICK, c.)

JACK. Since matters have come to this pass I demand an investigation.

PET. (*clasping her hands on his arm*). Yes! *We* demand an investigation.

BLAZ. (*aside*). Quite touching; but I will make her change her note. (*Aloud.*) Investigation, Mr. Ryder, is too formidable a word.

But if you will permit me to forget that I am your host, and ask—

DUCHESS. Permit you! A thief is obliged to answer what questions you choose.

PET. Jack, don't you speak a word!

BLAZ. It is in his own interest, Miss Seersucker.

JACK. Will you proceed with your questions, Lord Blazonberrie?

(DICK *enters*, C.)

BLAZ. The situation is novel. I hardly know how to begin.

DUCHESS. Demand the keys of his trunk, if you will begin at the beginning.

PET. Abominable! (*Goes to* R. F. *with* JACK; *sits by desk,* JACK *standing by her.* DUCHESS *sits,* L. F.; DICK *stands by fire.*)

BLAZ. (*stands,* C.). There is certainly a mystery, but it may be easily shown that it does not involve Mr. Ryder. (*To* JACK.) I think you have at no time been alone in this room, without witnesses, since the diamonds were placed in the safe?

JACK (*considering*). I cannot say that, Lord Blazonberrie.

BLAZ. Ah! May I ask at what hour you were alone here? You left Dick and myself in the dining-room half after nine, or thereabout.

JACK. When I left you I came here and found Miss Seersucker. Chetwyn joined us, and I went for a stroll in the park.

BLAZ. And that lasted—

DUCHESS. Any time he chooses to say. Why do you allow this adventurer to fabricate his story at his leisure?

BLAZ. This is hardly a scene for ladies. You and Miss Seersucker had best retire.

DUCHESS. I remain here.   .

PET. And I.

JACK. My stroll lasted twenty minutes or so. I returned, and found you with Miss Seersucker—

PET. Ah, I see!

JACK. —went out without disturbing you, came back about quarter-past ten—

DUCHESS (*rising*). It would be in order now, Mr. Ryder, to explain what was the magnet that brought you here again and again.

JACK (*taking no notice. She sits again*).

Chetwyn joined me, turned out the light, asked me to wait, went off. Suspecting a practical joke, I went to my room, packed my trunk, smoked a cigar, and retired about twelve o'clock.

BLAZ. Then you were alone here in the dark how long?

JACK. Possibly three minutes.

DUCHESS. That is when he took the diamonds! This accounts for his haste to leave us.

PET. A crime is not needed to explain that. I have felt the same desire myself. He might have been bored.

DUCHESS. It is a clear case. There is no other explanation.

BLAZ. Oh, good gad! (*Walks up and down.*)

PET. (*composedly*). Pardon, Duchess, but Englishwomen have been known to steal their own jewels, you know, when they or their sons have debts that cannot be acknowledged.

DUCHESS. You defend your accomplice with spirit, Miss Seersucker. (*Rises.*)

PET. (*springing up*). My accomplice!

JACK (*stepping forward*). Accomplice!

BLAZ. (*coming between*). I will not—

DUCHESS (*interrupting*). Let him explain why, having received neither letter nor telegram, he breaks up the dance for which he has ordered his costume, and is suddenly called away by business, of which he must have known when he accepted my invitation. (*Sits.*)

PET. Now, Jack. (*Sits.*)

JACK. I have nothing more to offer.

BLAZ. But surely, in consideration of the extraordinary situation, something more definite—if there were something.

JACK. There was, but it has no bearing on the case.

BLAZ. Still, it would serve you better to give it.

PET. (*aside*). That was a stab. He wishes to convict.

JACK (*steadily*). I have no more to offer.

DUCHESS. I insist that you send for the police, Blazonberrie.

BLAZ. Have you any theory, Mr. Ryder, as to who besides yourself could have learned the combination?

DICK. I say, Blazonberrie, don't your questions rather point one way?

Blaz. The answers do, perhaps, Dick.

Duchess. Precisely! The answers do.

Pet. (*indignantly*). Oh, oh!

Jack (*contemptuously*). Theory! There are a dozen. Some one may have listened behind the portières: some chance passer may have heard: the Duchess may have told some one—

Duchess. Who—I? When I could not remember the word?

Pet. You may have told, Duchess, and forgotten that and the word all in the one motion.

Duchess. Absurd!

Pet. It was a singular lapse of memory. Looks like a "put-up job," as they say in the States.

Blaz. (*hastily*). Did you see no one at all, meet no one, when you left it for the last time?

Jack. Why, yes, a servant — Robinson, I fancy—ran into me in the door.

Blaz. This was quarter-past ten, I think you said. (*Rings bell.*)

Jack. About that. (*Whispers to* Pet.)

(ROBINSON *enters*, C.)

ROB. Did you ring, my lord?

BLAZ. (*sitting on tête-à-tête*). Yes; we
have a joke, a bet, which I think you can
help us to decide. Were you in this room
last night?

ROB. I were, my lord. I brought your
lordship a letter, hand later I fetched a mes-
sage to Miss Seersucker from the Duchess.
Hit was hall dark, hand I lighted hup.

BLAZ. Was any one here?

ROB. I run hinto some one hin the door—
Mr. Ryder, I think—cos 'e says, 'urried like,
"No matter," wich your lordship hand Mr.
Dick most generally says— (*Hesitates.*)

BLAZ. Well?

ROB. Beg parding! But wen a body gets
hin your ways you says—ahem!—Damn you!

BLAZ. What time was this?

ROB. Quarter to heleven. I wound the
'all clock d'rectly hafterwards.

BLAZ. Quarter to eleven. Um! Was the
room quite as usual this morning?

ROB. The camery was pulled hout, hand
there was burnt matches by the desk, so

the 'ouse-maid she was, sure hit was burg-
lars— (*All exclaim "Oh!"*)

BLAZ. Go on.

ROB. But Saunders says Miss Tulu give
'im a plate to finish hup this morning, so we
suppoged heverything was hall right, hand
Mr. Dick 'ad been taking a picture. I 'ope
nothing his wrong.

BLAZ. Nothing. You may go.

ROB. (*taking amulet from his pocket*). We
found this little match-box like by the
desk. His hit yours, my lord? (*Hands him
amulet.*)

JACK. My amulet!

DUCHESS. By the desk! Blazonberrie—

BLAZ. Careful! Leave the room, Robinson.

ROB. Yes, my lord. (*Aside.*) Whathever is
going hon? (*Exit,* c.)

DUCHESS. Proof positive! And matches
burned by the safe. Blazonberrie, send for
the police.

JACK. I second the motion.

PET. Oh, Jack!

BLAZ. I cannot allow it.

JACK. But I insist. This examination is a

mere farce, and the circumstantial evidence proves nothing I wish to deny. I was alone here long enough to take the diamonds; I did lose my amulet; I did know the combination. On the other hand, it has yet to be *proved* that there is not in this house one who also knew the combination, and had a stronger motive than I for taking the jewels.

DUCHESS. Twenty thousand pounds is motive enough.

PET. Americans rate their good name higher, Duchess.

DUCHESS. How melodramatic!

BLAZ. I think I see a way out of the difficulty, if you will all leave me alone with Mr. Ryder.

DUCHESS. I shall write the Duke a letter giving all the facts, send it by messenger, and see if this delicate consideration for a thief meets his views. (*Exit*, c.)

DICK (*advancing*). Miss Seersucker, may I take you to the drawing-room?

PET. Yes. Courage, Jack! (*Exit with* DICK, L.)

BLAZ. (*after a moment's pause*). Mr. Ryder,

16

though I deprecate the Duchess's warmth, I
—I—

JACK. Share her sentiments. Well, the
evidence is strong. (*Lights cigarette, sits by
desk, facing* BLAZ., *who walks about, stopping
from time to time.*)

BLAZ. I— By Jove! put yourself in my
place.

JACK. Were I you I should have me ar-
rested.

BLAZ. I never was in such a dilemma.

JACK. Cut the Gordian knot; have me ar-
rested.

BLAZ. That is impossible, on Miss Seersucker's account. Standing in the position I
do to her—as—as her future husband—

JACK (*quietly*). As her future husband?

BLAZ. Yes. I am placed in a most awkward position. I cannot prosecute so near a
relative of my *fiancée;* neither can I refuse
to do so—my father could not—because these
jewels are entailed, and belong not to us, but
to the estate.

JACK. I see. What next? Shall I remove
the obstacle by hanging myself?

BLAZ. I do not understand your tone, Mr.

Ryder. I am very far from jesting. What I would say is this: either give me the necklace, or else slip quietly away now, while the others are not here. I promise you, on my honor, you shall not be followed.

Jack. Thanks. But how can you answer for that? The jewels are entailed; very good; then it is the duty of the Duke, your father, to regain possession of them.

Blaz. I tell you, you shall be safe — for Miss Seersucker's sake. We go deeper into these things than Americans do, and the Toedmags would not care to record an alliance with a felon's relative.

Jack. And we Americans go deeper yet. We never take refuge behind a petticoat. (*Rises.*)

Blaz. Then you refuse either to give up the jewels or go?

Jack. The jewels I have not got to give, and I most decidedly refuse to run away and bear the burden of another's crime.

Blaz. Whom do you suspect?

Jack. I will tell my counsel that.

Blaz. Suppose I decline and my father declines to prosecute?

JACK. You cannot. Remember the entail.

BLAZ. It may be evaded in some way.

JACK. Then I shall give myself up to the nearest magistrate.

BLAZ. Think of Miss Seersucker.

JACK. I do, but fancy she sees little to choose between a convict and an unconvicted thief, so prefer proving I am neither.

BLAZ. I must see her. This must not be. (*Goes to door,* L.) Miss Seersucker, may I speak with you a moment?

PET. (*entering,* L.). Speak with me? Certainly. (*Goes to* JACK; *holds out her hand.*) Jack!

JACK. Do not touch me! (*Crosses to door,* L.) Lord Blazonberrie, you will find me in here. (*Exit,* L.)

PET. What is the matter?

BLAZ. Your cousin is overwrought, Miss Seersucker. He is playing a desperate game.

PET. Desperate game! Then you believe him guilty?

BLAZ. I have fought against the idea, but he tacitly admits it himself. For your sake, I would never prosecute him, but I cannot hold back my family unless—unless—

PET. Well, my lord?

BLAZ. Unless you promise to marry me. Then, as cousin of my *fiancée*, he is safe.

PET. I see. (*Walks about.*)

BLAZ. Think of the position I am placed in. Forced to prosecute one who is not only near to you, but my friend and guest. Better lose a hundred thousand pounds, I say.

PET. And if I accept the condition, what next?

BLAZ. (*going to her*). Persuade him to leave here at once. He shall not be followed. I swear it.

PET. You want Jack to run away?

BLAZ. It is the only course. Urge it on him.

PET. Have you suggested it to him?

BLAZ. Yes, but he is determined to brazen it out. To you he must listen.

PET. Perhaps. (*Walks up and down; stops in front of* BLAZ.) Lord Blazonberrie, I accept your terms—

BLAZ. (*taking her hand*). My dear girl!

PET. (*releasing herself*). Wait! I accept, conditionally. (*With emphasis.*) On the day you convince me of Jack's guilt, I promise to marry you.

BLAZ. Then it is settled. And you will urge him to go at once?

PET. Send him to me, if you please.

BLAZ. (*kissing her hand*). You lift a load from my mind. (*Exit,* L.)

PET. (*rubbing her hand*). Faugh! His kiss burns. What hypocrites we women are! However, it is but fair. I do not quite believe in his disinterested care for me, nor do I like it. I am to get Jack out of his way, am I? Well, we will see.

(JACK *enters,* L.)

PET. Jack, I have a commission to execute. Will you please run away? Lord Blazonberrie most particularly requests it.

JACK. I dare say. Petrolia, before we go any further, I must know if it is true you are to marry Blazonberrie.

PET. I am—

JACK. Ah!

PET. Wait! only on the day he convinces me of your guilt, and that will be—never!

JACK. My darling Petrolia! (*Embraces her.*)

PET. How could you doubt me, Jack?

JACK. I was distracted with jealousy. Then came the accusation.

PET. Ah! the accusation! Jack, we must not waste time. You are innocent; then some one is guilty—some one in this house.

JACK. Whom do you suspect?

PET. The Duchess, or Blazonberrie, or both. (*Checks off points on her fingers.*) First point, the Duchess insists on telling you the combination ; second, she *forgets* it ; third, Blazonberrie brings out all the evidence against you; fourth, refuses you the benefit of a trial ; and fifth, uses every means in his power to induce you to run away.

JACK. Commend me to a woman's imagination !

PET. And me to a man's stupidity. But we must act, not talk. We will go to Blazonberrie, and again demand a trial.

JACK. And if he refuses I shall give myself up to Sir Henry Thornton, the nearest magistrate.

PET. I will drive over with you.

JACK. No, no.

PET. Yes, yes. Come, Jack, we must see Blazonberrie at once. (*They go off*, L.)

(T<small>ULU</small> *enters*, c., *carrying proof of photo.*)

T<small>ULU</small>. There's something queer going on, and I can't find out what it is. I thought it was funny Mr. Dick took me to his den to help Saunders. He wanted to get me out of the way. I made Saunders finish up *my* picture, and it is awfully funny, only no one will look at it. (*Sits on tête-à-tête; looks at picture.*) Oh, dear! I just wish some one would come; I'm dying to show it. Hateful things! always having secrets.

(*Enter* B<small>LAZONBERRIE</small>, c.)

T<small>ULU</small> (*running to him*). Lord Blazonberrie, I've got an awfully good joke on you. See! (*Holds out picture.*)

B<small>LAZ</small>. (*impatiently*). Don't be a nuisance! Where is your sister?

T<small>ULU</small>. Find her yourself. (B<small>LAZ</small>. *goes off*, L.) "Don't be a nuisance!" Indeed! I am a nuisance, am I? Well, they can keep their old secret. I've one of my own.

(*Enter* D<small>ICK</small>.)

T<small>ULU</small>. Oh, Mr. Dick! (*Puts picture behind her.*)

DICK. Holloa, Tulu! (*Throws himself on sofa.*)

TULU. Holloa yourself! I'm not a baby.

DICK. Pardon my disrespect, Miss. I'm all out of sorts. Blue as indigo.

TULU. Does your poor head ache?

DICK. Like thunder.

TULU. Then I'll cologne it. (*Puts picture on table, takes scent bottle from her pocket, goes to Dick.*) Put your head back. (*Rubs his head.*)

DICK. You're a good sort, Tulu.

TULU. Does it make you worse to talk?

DICK. No; but I can't be larky.

TULU. Of course not when you're blue. I'm never blue myself, but I'm blaze.

DICK. What's that last word?

TULU. Blaze. It's French for sort of tired of things. When I go to matinées I hardly cry a bit. I've seen it all before, you know. Don't you know French?

DICK. Not as intimately as you do.

TULU. I guess you're chaffing. I say, Mr. Dick, you didn't take a picture last night, did you?

DICK. No.

Tulu. But you fixed the camera for one, didn't you?

Dick. Yes, but my subject got away.

Tulu. Mine didn't—at least, I caught another, and took a picture that's a regular Jim dandy.

Dick. Didn't I tell you not to meddle with my camera? (*Sits up.*)

Tulu. Put your head back. (*He does so.*) I didn't meddle at all. The machine was in order, so I just meant to snap you off for fun.

Dick. Well, you didn't get me.

Tulu. I got something better yet. The queerest thing you ever did see. I'll show it to you. Just a little more cologne. (*Tilts bottle over his head.*)

Dick (*jumping up*). Oh, my eye! Oh!

Tulu. Oh, I'm so sorry! I'll fetch some water. (*Runs to door, c.*)

Dick. You'll fetch nothing! (*Jostles her in door, runs off, holding handkerchief to his eye.*)

Tulu. What an awful day I'm having! (*Feels her elbow.*) He nearly broke my arm, and didn't even see the picture. (*Catches up picture.*) Oh, dear, I wish I was home! I do. (*Flings herself on sofa.*) Everybody is just perfectly hateful! (*Sobs.*)

(*Enter* PETROLIA, L.)

PET. Tulu in tears! Poor little thing, she has heard the news. (*Goes to her.*) What is the matter, Tulu? (*Kneels by sofa.*)

TULU. Mr. Dick wouldn't look at my picture. I wish I was dead!

PET. Is that all? Tulu, dear, I want you to go up-stairs at once, and help Parker pack our boxes. We leave here to-day.

TULU (*sitting up*). Have you had a row with the Duchess, Smithy?

PET. (*sitting by her*). Yes.

TULU. Then I'll stay and see the thing out.

PET. Please go, like a dear girl.

TULU. I'm not a dear girl. I'm a nuisance. I want to be a nuisance. No one will oblige me by looking at my picture, and I won't oblige any one.

PET. I'll look at the picture if you'll only go away. (*Holds out her hand.*)

TULU. It's a joke—don't grab it! There! (*Gives her photo.*) Isn't that capital? What

do you s'pose he is doing?   Saunders and I
nearly had a fit over it.

PET. It's Lord Blazonberrie!

TULU. Yes, and he's holding a necklace—
see!

PET. (*springing up. Goes to light*). The
Ranee's necklace! Tulu, how did you get
this picture?

TULU. Last night. I was waiting to get
Mr. Dick, you know—

PET. Yes; go on.

TULU. I turned out the light, crawled behind the table with the bulb in my hand, and
went to sleep. Well—

PET. Do hurry, Tulu.

TULU. Well, I don't know how long I slept
—not long, I guess. Anyway, I waked up,
and heard some one sneaking to the door.
Of course I thought it was Dick, so I squeezed
the bulb, and the flash went off.

PET. Yes; and then?

TULU. Then I pulled out the plate, wrapped
it up in the cloth, and took it up to bed with
me. And this morning when Saunders de-
veloped it it was Blazonberrie, not Dick.
Isn't it funny?

PET. Funny ? It's adorable ! (*Kisses* TULU.)
Tulu, you've saved us.

TULU. What ever has got into you ?

(*Enter* DUCHESS, BLAZONBERRIE, *and* DICK, C.)

DUCHESS. Where is Mr. Ryder ? Did no
one watch him ?

PET. I did, Duchess.

BLAZ. And he has gone ?

(JACK *enters*, L.)

JACK. I am still here, Lord Blazonberrie.
Have you any more evidence, Duchess ?

DUCHESS. No. Blazonberrie—

PET. One moment, Duchess. Lord Blazonberrie, I cry off from our bargain. So
far from being convinced of my cousin's
guilt, I have proof positive of his inno-
cence.

DUCHESS. Bargain ? What bargain ?

JACK. Petrolia ! What is—

DUCHESS (*interrupting*). The proofs first,
if you please.

PET. You may not like them, Duchess.
Lord Blazonberrie, what do you say ?

BLAZ. What have I to do with the matter?

PET. (*holding out photo to* DICK). Mr. Chetwyn, will you look at this picture, and tell us who it is?

DICK (*taking it*). Blazonberrie! Splendid! Perfect! Who took this?

TULU (*proudly*). I did. Thought I was going to spoil your camera if I touched it!

PET. (*earnestly*). Mr. Chetwyn, what does Lord Blazonberrie hold in his hand?

DICK (*looking*). The Ranee's necklace; no one could mistake that pendant. (*Starts.*) By Jove! when was this taken?

TULU. Last night, about eleven o'clock.

ALL. Eleven o'clock!

TULU. Yep; eleven o'clock. (*Laughs.*)

BLAZ. (*aside*). The flash! Oh, double-dyed fool!

JACK. Tulu! You took Lord Blazonberrie with the Ranee's necklace in his hand at eleven o'clock last night?

TULU. Yep, and never knew it — there's where the joke comes in. I was laying for Mr. Dick in the dark, and was sleepy—it was awfully hot; I was behind the table there—

so I dropped off in a little nap. Well, I had the bulb all ready, waked up, heard some one in the room, thought it was Mr. Dick, squeezed the bulb, and never knew till this morning what I had got. Isn't it grand? Mr. Dick never got anything half as good. Isn't it a joke on him?

DICK. It's a serious sort of joke on us all, Tulu.

DUCHESS (*seizing picture*). It is Blazonberrie! But it proves nothing. It is an American trick.

TULU. Trick! I tell you—

PET. (*interrupting*). Tulu, this is serious. Last night the Ranee's necklace was stolen—

TULU. Stolen! Stolen here! Was I alone in the room with a real burglar? (*Looks at* BLAZ.) Oh! Oh! Lord Blazonberrie had the necklace. Petrolia, what have I done?

JACK. Saved my reputation. They accused me—

PET. Yes, Tulu, they called Jack a thief!

DUCHESS. And do still. It is a conspiracy.

DICK. Aunt Hildegarde, be reasonable.

JACK. Very good. I return to my first proposition : order my arrest.

BLAZ. Stuff! Nonsense! I have been a fool, but know when the game is up. I overheard the combination, and stole my own diamonds. There you have it. We will say nothing, and you will say nothing, for we might still make it unpleasant for you, in spite of Tulu and her camera. (*Goes over to fire.*)

DUCHESS. Wretched boy! he confesses his disgrace! (*Sits,* L. F.)

DICK (*going to her*). Aunt Hildegarde, we owe Mr. Ryder a most humble apology.

DUCHESS. Not at all. It was but natural to think twenty thousand pounds a great temptation to a man of his stamp. (*Fans herself violently.*)

TULU. You're off about his " stamp," Duchess. Blazonberrie is a gentleman because he couldn't help being born a Toedmag; but Jack is a gentleman because he likes to be. So there!

PET. My dear Tulu—

TULU. You can't down me, Smithy. It's the solid truth I'm giving her.

JACK (*kissing her*). You are a little trump.

TULU. But I take a big trick, don't I?

TABLEAU.

BLAZONBERRIE.   PETROLIA.   DICK.
       TULU.   DUCHESS.
         JACK.

ROB. (*entering*, c.). The carriage waits, Miss Seersucker.

QUICK CURTAIN.

17

BY MARY E. WILKINS.

A New England Nun, and Other Stories. 16mo, Cloth, Ornamental, $1 25. (*Just published.*)

A Humble Romance, and Other Stories. 16mo, Cloth, Extra, $1 25.

Only an artistic hand could have written these stories, and they will make delightful reading.—*Evangelist*, N. Y.

The simplicity, purity, and quaintness of these stories set them apart in a niche of distinction where they have no rivals.—*Literary World*, Boston.

The reader who buys this book and reads it will find treble his money's worth in every one of the delightful stories.—*Chicago Journal.*

Miss Wilkins is a writer who has a gift for the rare art of creating the short story which shall be a character study and a bit of graphic picturing in one ; and all who enjoy the bright and fascinating short story will welcome this volume.—*Boston Traveller.*

The author has the unusual gift of writing a short story which is complete in itself, having a real *beginning*, a *middle*, and an *end*. The volume is an excellent one.—*Observer*, N. Y.

A gallery of striking studies in the humblest quarters of American country life. No one has dealt with this kind of life better than Miss Wilkins. Nowhere are there to be found such faithful, delicately drawn, sympathetic, tenderly humorous pictures.—*N. Y. Tribune.*

The charm of Miss Wilkins's stories is in her intimate acquaintance and comprehension of humble life, and the sweet human interest she feels and makes her readers partake of, in the simple, common, homely people she draws.—*Springfield Republican.*

There is no attempt at fine writing or structural effect, but the tender treatment of the sympathies, emotions, and passions of no very extraordinary people gives to these little stories a pathos and human feeling quite their own.—*N. Y. Commercial Advertiser.*

The author has given us studies from real life which must be the result of a lifetime of patient, sympathetic observation. . . . No one has done the same kind of work so lovingly and so well.—*Christian Register*, Boston.

Published by HARPER & BROTHERS, New York.